DISGRACED

A CASEY CORT LEGAL THRILLER

AIME AUSTIN

AIME AUSTIN
www.AimeAustin.com

LOS ANGELES, CALIFORNIA

DISGRACED

A CASEY CORT LEGAL THRILLER

AIME AUSTIN

Disgraced

This edition published by
Moore Digital Media Inc.
1125 N Fairfax Avenue
Unit 46071
West Hollywood, CA 90046
www.*aimeaustin*.com

Cover Designer: Wicked Good Book Covers
Cover images © Depositphotos, Shutterstock

Disgraced/Aime Austin. — 2d ed.

Whereof what's past is prologue;
what to come, in yours and my discharge.

William Shakespeare — *The Tempest*, Act 2, Scene I.

1

"What did you want?" Lulu Mueller asked. She gave me a look of pure disbelief.

"I...um...thought I could borrow your computer for a couple of minutes," I replied, awkwardly stumbling over my answer. I wasn't so dense I didn't know that ball gowns and email didn't mix.

"Why?"

From my spot on Lulu's office chair in her bedroom, I leaned over the sparkly beaded purse to the overnight bag I'd used to bring my gown to my best friend's house. From a side pocket, I fished out a three-and-a-half inch floppy disk. I held up the gray plastic so my friend could see the sticker I'd carefully labeled months ago.

"Second Year Comments," she read. "You've got to be kidding. This ball, all of this," she gestured to her half made up face, "was your idea. Now, you want to do work?"

"I'll be quick, I swear. It's a memo I'm supposed to send out. Plus you still have to finish getting ready."

"Because I didn't spend my day at a spa in Beachwood."

"Tom mentioned tonight being special. If what's gonna happen is what I think is gonna happen, a girl's gotta turn herself into a swan." I circled my index finger around my made up face and blown out hair. "This is Tom Brody we're talking about. He could have any girl he wants in the five county area."

"Fine." Lulu huffed, but took herself back to the en suite bathroom. "What in the hell is so important, you have to send it now?" Her question echoed off the tiles.

"It's a general progress report. I'm supposed to give the second-years general and specific feedback on their law review comments. This is their second draft, and they're still mostly shit."

"Not everyone is in it to win it, Casey." Lulu popped her head back in and she was looking a bit more evened out, a bit less like Batman's nemesis, Two Face.

"Law review is the most prestigious thing you can do in law school. If these kids want to splash journal membership over their resume fifty different times, then they should do the work. It's not some popularity contest."

The computer took its time coming to life. When the desktop finally came into view, I double-clicked on the icon that would connect me to the school. The crackling sound of the modem filled the room then dissipated as I made a successful connection.

Careful of my manicure, I double-clicked on her mouse, opening the Word Perfect file and looked at the memo one more time. I didn't know Lulu was reading over my shoulder until her breath stirred the straight hair laying down my back.

"Hey," I said, swatting at her. "I don't want it going curly again."

Lulu sat heavily on her bed. The frothy pink and white four-poster stood in stark contrast to the purple and black striped walls and homegrown rap group posters.

"Have we ever had the discussion about tact?" Lulu broached.

As always, I resisted pointing out that telling it like it was all the time to everyone was the opposite of tact as well.

"Not this again," I said, sighing. I swiveled in the chair to face her. "These are not babies. If they can't take the heat..." I left the rest unsaid. From where I was sitting, colleges and now even law schools were doing way too much coddling and not enough straight talking.

Lulu pulled her glasses from atop her head, and smashed them down onto her nose. She read from my memo.

"Do not use passive voice. Do not improperly use words. Do not make unsubstantiated statements. Do not plagiarize. Do not ignore the foregoing rules. If you do not heed them, you will not produce a publishable comment. You will not elevate."

Lulu pushed her glasses back up and sat down heavily on her skull-covered duvet. Her sigh was heavy, world weary, overwrought.

"What?" I swiveled to face her again.

She was silent for a beat.

"Just say it."

"You used 'foregoing' and 'heed' in a single memo," Lulu said as if I'd used curse words.

"Your point?"

"This is not win friends and influence people language. More like alienate people and piss them off language."

"They turned in shit, Lulu. Unsubstantiated, derivative shit. I swear they should have to elevate before being able to put law review on their resume. It's like they got on the review, slapped it on some heavy cream stock, then ran out to on-campus interviews with their shiny new accomplishment. Actually working on a journal that has to publish six issues a year doesn't seem to be in the picture for these people."

I turned back to the computer, clicked send, then shut it down. I was done thinking about law school for a night. Tom and graduation and what all that meant about the future needed my complete focus and concentration.

Whatever else Lulu was going to say was cut off when her mom came in, designer shoeboxes in hand. I was suddenly very glad my best friend, her mother, and I both wore a size seven-and-a-half shoe.

"You cleaned up...surprisingly...well."

That was one of my co-editors, Roxy Wyles, giving me the most backhanded of compliments. Roxy, Lulu, and I were in the bathroom of the Lakewood Country Club. Outside the heavy wood door, The Advocates Ball, our law schools class' answer to the senior prom was getting started.

"You think?" I did a quick twirl in my pale blue halter dress. It had set me back a real pretty penny at Dillard's. But I planned to pay off the charges I was racking with this ball and my graduation expenses come fall.

Morrell, Gates & Noble's first year salary, which would yield me a cool seventy thousand dollars, would have me covered. More than covered. It was above and beyond what my parents had probably ever made in any year, and they'd bought a house and raised me. In impossibly high heels, Roxy teetered off to powder her nose or something.

"I can't believe we're here," Lulu whispered. A few of our classmates' dates had come into the room, their giggles and gossip drowning out our voices. The placard on the door that had read 'Women's Lounge' was a one hundred percent accurate description. It was more living room than ladies room. Plush leather chairs, a basket of designer perfumes, and soft-looking tissues filled the bathroom. There wasn't a toilet or sink in sight. Done scanning the room, taking in what would be my future, I turned back to Lulu.

"Tom really wanted me to come," I said. I wasn't a formal party kind of person, but my boyfriend was. So I'd dragged my best friend to the ball as well.

"You think he's going to pop the question?" Lulu asked, grabbing and shaking my arm insistently.

I didn't answer while peeling her fingers from my skin. Instead, I looked away, trying to hide my longing. I hoped more than anything there was a diamond in my immediate future. After spending half of last week shopping for this new dress and new underwear to go with it, I'd burned through the rest of my credit limit on a manicure, pedicure, and blowing out my hair. It was the first time in my life someone other than me had painted my fingernails and toenails, or had made my curly flyaway hair runway model smooth.

I'd done my part, now I was ready for Tom to do his. Like a movie, I could envision Tom tapping on the mike at the front of the room, getting the band to play something appropriately sappy. Then a spotlight would shine down on him as he came to me on bended knee. The ring would sparkle like fire under the lights. All my classmates would applaud for the desirable girl, the girl every guy in the room was sorry he'd overlooked. I'd stop being the ambitious girl who had clawed her way onto the law review masthead and into the inner sanctum of a white shoe firm.

"You're thinking about that ring, aren't you?" Lulu demanded. That question brought me back down to earth from my daydream and tuned me back in to the world around me.

"Your outfit turned out...nice," I said, watching Lulu touch up her hot pink lipstick.

"I look like an extra from Sixteen Candles," Lulu said.

Our eyes met in the mirror and I couldn't help laughing. She was totally right. Lulu Mueller had what I always thought of as...eclectic taste. On most days, she looked like a rap video reject. Tonight the sequins on her dress competed for glitter champion with the sparkling cat-eye glasses that were her favorite accessory. Maybe a Madonna or Cyndi Lauper video girl more than John Hughes actress.

"You didn't have to come," I said.

"You're so full of shit. You practically twisted my arm. So here I am with the dastardly Jason Sullivan."

"Is he that bad?" I hoped he wasn't that bad. He was one of Tom's good friends. One of his rich inner circle. When James had asked Lulu, I thought it would be perfect. We could double date, and if Tom popped the question, at least my best friend would be there to witness it.

"It'll be fine. I don't have to marry Jason. We'll drink. I'll dance. He'll bore me to death with cases from securities law, and the night will end in," Lulu checked the tiny gold watch her mom had lent her, "T minus four hours."

Once Lulu had put the nearly neon lipstick back in her bag, I linked my elbow with hers and escorted her out of the lounge door.

"Let's get some wine," she suggested. It was the best idea of the night so far.

We came back to the ten-person table, wine in hand.

Tom stood and pulled out my chair. I nearly died from the chivalry. When he wanted to, when he made even the tiniest effort, my boyfriend could be the absolute best. "I hope you guys didn't talk about us too bad in there."

I leaned over and laid my lips on Tom's smooth cheek. He smelled like some kind of spice, cloves maybe. I loved that smell.

"Nothing too embarrassing," I said, and then winked at him.

"Where are you after graduation?" Jason Sullivan asked before my butt could even hit the chair properly. He hadn't taken a page from Tom's playbook, and Lulu was doing the best she could to scoot into her own seat without catching her hem on a chair leg.

"Morrell Gates," I finally answered, nearly as proud of that name as I was of my own.

"That's right," Jason said, leaning back in contemplation like he was a man twice his age. "I remember now. Tom got you an interview at one of the biggies. Good for you."

"Ah Jason, my dad got her the interview. She got the job on her own smarts," Tom interjected.

It still burned a little that my top of the class grades and law review credentials hadn't been enough to get in the door at Morrell. My mother said it didn't matter what opened the door, it only mattered that I'd proven myself last summer enough to earn an offer.

Done with me, Jason turned to Lulu. "And you're going to Dalton Lacey down the street." When Lulu made no move to respond, he looked from me to her and back again. "Cozy."

"Are you looking forward to going in-house with the new women's NBA team?" I asked to spare Lulu the tiring job of being Jason Sullivan's sole entertainment. I'd thought about pretending I had no idea of Sullivan's plans, but that would have been a shit thing to do. There wasn't anyone within earshot of this country club who didn't know he was going in-house with Cleveland's latest sports team, a WNBA franchise scheduled to start up in the city next year.

Sullivan, a tall Irish kid, who'd probably slept with a Larry Bird pillow until he was eighteen, enthused about basketball and what a women's basketball franchise would mean for the city for a good half hour. I could see Lulu taking sneak peeks at her watch when she thought no one was looking.

Openly, I looked at my own watch. T minus three-and-a-half.

Dancing had never been one of my skills, but I was thrilled when the music changed from orchestral to Top Forty and drowned out the talk of career plans. The lights dimmed just that bit more, and Tom leaned closer. I nearly fell off my chair in anticipation.

"It's a special night," he said. Those were exactly the right words. I waited with bated breath for more, but nothing else followed.

"I'm glad I came," I said, prompting him. And I was, finally, glad that I'd come around to the idea of a gown and a country club and all the pomp and circumstance involved in dressing up to hang out with people you saw every day because the payoff was just around the corner.

I half wondered if he'd buy me some brand new ring from that jewelry store we'd once visited on Mayfield Road oh-so-conveniently located across from the bridal store, or if there were some kind of family ring passed down through generations of Brodys that I'd wake up to on my finger tomorrow morning.

"There's something I want to ask you," Tom said.

I fought to hear him over the roar of anticipation in my ears.

It was coming.

Finally.

The night I'd been waiting for, patiently, for two and a half years. This would be the day we cemented the plans we'd been dancing around for months. This would be the day I was going to become the fiancé of one Tom Brody.

In six months, I could stand next to Tom at the Supreme Court swearing in ceremony, my ring winking in the camera flash as I held up my bar certificate in family photos.

Bryan Adams' 'Heaven' came from the cover band on the small raised stage.

I took a deep breath.

I was ready.

"Anything, Tom," I said. I wanted him to know that I'd say yes to whatever he asked.

"Dance with me."

I stood, letting my date, handsome as ever in his tuxedo lead me to the miniature parquet dance floor set up in front of the band. Privacy, of course. I should have realized a guy like him would have wanted that. Needed that. He wasn't the type to propose between chardonnay and WNBA chat.

We didn't possess any moves between us, but we swayed to the music nonetheless.

"You had something you wanted to ask me?" I prompted again. Tom's barely discernible wince, told me I was graceless. Between him and Lulu, I was thinking finishing school wouldn't be out of place.

"I asked you, dear pretty lady, to dance with me," he said, whirling us in complete three sixty.

Spinning and white wine didn't mix. I gulped air to keep Lulu's mom's rugelah down.

I turned my head, laying my cheek against his chest. I didn't want him to see my disappointment. I wasn't owed an engagement. He'd said just last weekend that he couldn't wait for us to share a future. That would have to be enough for now.

Bryan Adams faded, and the band announced a break. Music from a low-key mixtape came through the speakers. I lifted my head, ready to go back to the table or the buffet of appetizers. A lot of other students had gone out to a pre-dance dinner, but Tom had had some kind of family obligation. Lulu and I had skipped the meal—all the better to fit into our dresses—but wine on top of a couple of cookies and dancing was making my head feel like it could float away from my body at any moment.

Before I could make jamming some kind of sauerkraut ball or sausage stuffed mushrooms into my mouth a priority, Tom steered me toward a side door that led out to a little terrace. Forty-degree weather nipped at my bare arms.

"I did want to ask you something, just not in there."

The chill that had goose bumped my skin a moment ago eased. In its place, heat flushed my chest and neck. I didn't need a mirror to know it was creeping up my face as well. I hoped the sweat prickling my scalp didn't curl my hair.

Here it was.

"Yes," I said peremptorily. "Yes, to whatever you ask."

Tom stepped back. Damn. I'd jumped the gun. Again. Somehow, with Tom, my timing was never right. Two years later, and I was still awkward and out of sorts when he was within a few feet of me.

His laugh was awkward. Shit. What had I stepped into?

"Glad to have your agreement. That's really a load off."

"What did I agree to?" I asked. I was still half hoping, despite the mounting evidence to the contrary that this night would end with a diamond ring on my finger.

"You know Ted Strohmeyer's going to be starting his second year at Morrell Gates in September."

It took me a full minute to process Tom's sentence. The four words 'will you marry me' had been nowhere in his statement. Like the good little lawyer I was training to be, I turned off the emotion in my brain and went for the sensible.

"He was in the summer class the year before us. I maybe saw him a couple of times last summer," I said. Diplomatic is what that statement had been. Ted had drunk and fucked his way through his summer. I'd heard more than once that he'd drunk with the partners and fucked their secretaries. He'd never completed any of the assignments that had been thinly disguised tests to see if we could survive as first year lawyers playing with the big dogs.

If you believed the gossip mill, his first year had been a lot more of the same.

No one in our small summer class was surprised he was still around, though. When your dad owned the one brewery that was still in business a few recessions later, no law firm would turn down the scion that could represent millions of dollars of business. If it were a choice between Strohmeyer and me, even I knew that even if I worked three thousand hours a year, they'd pick him.

"He's a great family friend, you know."

I did know that. We'd been out with Ted and his girl-friend of the night more times than I'd enjoyed. He made Jason Sullivan look like a raconteur. But I considered all of it—Sullivan, Strohmeyer, the rest of the boors and bores—practice. I knew when Tom and I got married, there'd be many nights like that one down the line where being nice would earn us more than brownie points.

"What do you, or does he, need?"

"His dad was at dinner tonight. It's why I couldn't do the meal thing with Lulu and Jason. Family only. You under-stand."

I didn't quite understand how long it would be before I crossed that threshold, could attend the family dinners, but I stood mute waiting for the rest.

"Edward, Ted's dad, is kind of worried that Ted may not make it through his second year at Morrell Gates. It's im-portant to the Strohmeyers that he stay on there for a few years."

"So..." I said. Because other than doing Ted Strohmeyer's job for him, I had no idea how in the hell I could help.

"So, Ed asked if I knew anyone from Cleveland-Marshall who'd be at the firm. I told him that my very smart girl-friend Casey Cort would be starting there as a first-year."

"And…" Whether it was nerves or hunger, I couldn't tell, but the longer Tom drew out his request, the more uneasy my stomach became.

"Can you kind of keep an eye on him?"

"How? He's a grown man who will, from what I hear, do whatever he likes."

"Look. If he's fucking around too much, please tell me. You're entering labor and employment, right?"

"That's the plan."

"He's in corporate now. But I looked up the firm. There aren't that many corporate partners. Maybe you could, I don't know, help him with his assignments, let me know if he gets too off track."

I suppressed a flash of irritation. A marriage proposal this was not. I didn't like to say no to people, especially Tom, but…

"I can probably let you know on that first thing. Law firms are nothing if not gossip machines. But Ted will be in an entirely different department. I really have no way of knowing how or what he'll be doing. I mean, this summer, we got to spend time in all the departments; litigation, labor and employment, tax, and corporate. I don't know how much crossover there will be between labor and his department." That wasn't entirely true; there was plenty of crossover between us and them. Half of the labor work came from corporate, but what he was asking was more than I wanted to handle.

"Gotcha." His tone was dismissive, his square jaw set in displeasure.

"It's not like the prosecuting attorney's office," I started to explain. "You guys will probably be working more closely together there."

Tom nodded thoughtfully. Despite a years-long hiring freeze, Tom's uncle, or father, or brother had made sure there was a spot for him in the county's biggest public law firm—prosecuting crimes.

"It's like a three-hundred attorney firm." I gave further explanation. I wanted Tom to know I was there for him. There if his family needed me. But this was one thing I couldn't really do. "We were all together this summer doing drinks, dinner, Indians games. But come fall, we'll be shuttled off to different departments. Except for seeing you, I don't think I'll be outside of the library or whatever little cubicle they shoehorn me into." Firms, especially top tier, white shoe firms like Morrell Gates weren't known for their flexibility.

"It was just an idea. Obviously, something I didn't think over too much. But consider what I said. It's really important to the family. And one day soon, you'll be part of that family. You'll understand better then, why things like this are important."

So marriage was still on the table. But not today. Relief flowed through me. I'd be ready next time. I shivered. Barely above freezing temps and bare arms didn't mix.

"Damn. Sorry. Let's go in." Tom laid a hand on my waist. I wanted to curl into that arm, wrap it around me, have him hold me for a kiss. But we didn't have that kind of relationship. Tom wasn't into public displays, and coming from a prominent family, I understood that. His, and Ted Strohmeyer's, for that matter. Cleveland was a medium-sized city, but at the very top where their families hovered above the rest of us, every move was probably watched by someone who would report back to his dad, brother, uncle, or cousins.

His hand brushed against my hip. The next shiver wasn't because of the cold. It was because I hoped against hope that Tom would come back to my apartment after the ball and maybe we could make love, have sex, make out, I don't know, something, anything that would let me know that Tom still desired me.

I knew that I wasn't the most beautiful woman in the world, nowhere color hair, too much in the hip department, especially if I didn't watch what I ate, but I wanted my future husband to want me. Not in the way that romance heroes couldn't get enough of their fiery, sassy heroines. But in the way real men loved their women, a little bit more than he loved me now.

"Why don't you sit? Let me get you a plate," Tom said, pulling out my chair at the table. I sat, closing the wrap around me that I should have taken outside. He made his way over to the food.

Lulu leaned way over the empty chair between us. She waggled her left hand at me, tapping her fourth finger with her thumb. The question in that movement was obvious. As subtly as I could, I shook my head. "Later," I mouthed. Maybe she could help me make sense of Tom's request, because I surely couldn't.

2

All right people, I know we're all ready to get our ham on. I have to get to my mom's house for her überbacken." I loved the tomato, cheese and fish bake my mom always made for Good Friday. Celebrating Easter with my parents would be far better than herding cats in the law review office. But, I was finding, the work of Executive Comment Editor was never done. Being on the masthead wasn't just for show.

"Why are we here exactly, Casey?" one editor asked, shifting in his seat. There were nine other editors sitting around the conference table, including Erwin Gesick, my boss, the law review's editor-in-chief. They all looked at me, their patience on an early Friday afternoon paper-thin.

"Doesn't anyone read the memos I write?" I asked. I always detailed the reason for a meeting in an agenda I circulated a week before.

"Maybe you can call it senioritis," one editor said, laughing. "But no one here's working too hard. We have one month until we're outta here. Then the bar, then work."

"Yeah, the law review's done what it needed to do, filled our resumes and got most of us jobs," another lobbed across the room. He was reclined so far back in his chair, I could barely see him.

"Let's make it quick, then," I said. "It's my job as Senior Comment Editor to decide what or if we're going to include our own writing in next year's journal. Like we did this year, the next batch of editors will publish six student articles."

That got their attention. Roxy Wyles, the only other woman in the room, started pointing her finger around the room. Her lips moved silently.

"There are nine of us," she said, all done with counting. "There are only six slots for our notes. How are we going to decide?"

"It's not just nine comments, Roxy. Actually, there are a total of fifteen comments under submission. Everyone was required to write one last year. So this is where reading the memo comes in," I said. "I think we should do something different this year."

All eyes focused on me, but maybe not in a good way. Except for Gesick, there was a lot of grumbling and shifting in the seats. Even the editor who'd been leaning back like our office was his bedroom sprang up.

"There are those from editors on the articles side of the law review." I hefted a stack from the table. "Not counting mine, that makes a total of fourteen submissions. There are still only six slots."

"So, what? We vote on who gets in?"

"That's what happened last year," I said. "And maybe before, I don't know." I shrugged. "Look, a lot of you have complained in meetings that you'd like our journal to be taken more seriously. To be quoted as much as Harvard or Yale or Chicago. I agree. I want all this ass busting work we've done over the last eighteen months to really mean something." I took a deep breath before I got to the part they weren't going to like. "I'm proposing that we recuse ourselves from consideration for Volume Forty-five."

That woke them up. Suddenly it went from creakingly quiet chairs to everyone speaking at once.

"I ran for office for one reason: to get my comment published in the law review. I had no burning desire to read boring ass student crap or check citations." Roxy was the first to say what I assumed everyone thought.

"I ran for office, and won, by the way, to raise the standard of writing for the law review. I've been working with the second-years since last summer. They're going to have some kick ass comments next year. They'll be published everywhere, probably bump up our ranking."

"That's all well and good for you, Casey. You have a job at Morrell Gates, and you've practically married into the biggest judicial family in the freaking state," Roxy said.

I shifted my eyes away from the pale brunette. She'd been in competition with me from day one. She'd gone on a date with Tom, but he'd never asked for a second. She'd been turned down for a job with Morrell. I think she'd ended up working for free for some government agency. Then she'd run against me for Senior Comment Editor. Needless to say, she hadn't won.

"So, to get the ball rolling, I'm pulling my comment from consideration. I got a letter just this week. It's been accepted by the Journal of Feminist Jurisprudence."

Groans and eye-rolling followed.

"I'm sure getting published there was difficult," one editor said.

"Catherine MacKinnon and Susan Estrich must have taken the month off," said another.

"Probably on the rag." That was from a third.

I rolled my neck. Fucking men. The law school was oozing with testosterone. It leeched around every corner like the Blob. Tom was probably the only sane one in the bunch. The rest of the knuckle draggers were out for themselves and nothing more. Just like Jason Sullivan. Just like Ted Strohmeyer. They wanted all the prestige with none of the work.

Our fearless leader Gesick rapped on the faux wood table with his knuckles. "Your efforts are admirable, Casey," he said. I waited a beat for the big old 'but' that was coming. "But, you need to understand that the rest of us want a chance to be published in a real law journal. Now, I say we take a vote on whether to pull our comments from submission to the law journal."

I watched Gesick usurp my meeting.

"All in favor?"

My hand was the sole limb in the air.

"That, Casey, is the democratic process in action," Gesick said. "Now all those who'd like to submit their comments for publication, leave five copies in my mailbox. I'm sure Casey will be happy to set up a meeting after the Easter break to see who we'll publish in next year's issues. Now, let's get to the ham."

"I'll second that," Wyles said.

Everyone except Gesick bundled up and took a quick exit.

"What was that all about?" he asked as we walked from the law review office to the tiny room for the three top officers on the masthead shared.

"I thought we wanted to be taken seriously," I said, unlocking the door.

"You think it's any different at Columbia or Northwestern?"

"Those schools are in the top tier. They can kind of do anything. I wanted our students to spread their wings. Stand out on their merits. If we were published widely, then maybe people would stand up and take note of Cleveland-Marshall. Just because we're a state school in a small city, doesn't mean we can't be good lawyers, I don't know, make some kind of change in the world."

"Are you going to take that idealism to Morrell Gates?"

"Client representation is different, I know that. But they do have a pro bono program that I'm really looking forward to digging into."

Gesick stood and walked over to me. He yoked an arm around my shoulder and pulled me into an embrace. The kiss he planted on my temple was unexpected. Lulu had said the editor-in-chief had a crush on me, but I'd dismissed that. Who constantly patronized someone they had interest in? We weren't kindergarteners on the schoolyard where a boy hit you if he liked you.

"I'll be down the road in Canton. If Tom never does the right thing and proposes, I'll be happy to spring for dinner." It was the first flat-out invitation.

I was sometimes oblivious, but I wasn't stupid. Stupid hadn't put me at the top of my class or in the Senior Comment Editor position. Awkward advances, though, were hard to handle.

"It's only a matter of time before we're engaged. Thanks, though."

"I'm not sure you're Tom's type," he whispered. Gesick's breath made me shiver uncomfortably. Finally, he unwound his arm from me. "Offer's open. Want me to walk you out?"

"Going to do a little work on the next issue before I head home," I said. "It's only twelve-thirty. My mom won't expect me before five or so."

"Suit yourself."

Defeated, I retreated to my desk in the office that Gesick and I had shared for the last eight months. I tossed out the memo no one had bothered to read and plopped into my chair. There were going to be two student comments in the upcoming issue. It would come out in the fall long after we'd graduated, but it was our responsibility nonetheless.

I looked at the wall clock, its tick tock the loudest sound in the nondescript room. Two hours. That was how long I'd give to this today. I'd skim the comments, pick the two best, and be done with it. I'd tried my best. It was all I could do. I'd have law review on my resume for the rest of my life.

Morrell Gates or any future employer wouldn't give a crap about my reform efforts. Neither would Tom. The future with my firm and my soon-to-be fiancé was what mattered. The Cleveland Law Review had existed before me, and would continue long thereafter. I'd probably been overreaching to think that I could make change at the law school, make us a little more relevant in the legal community.

I picked up and sipped at a long ago abandoned coffee that I fervently hoped was mine, and got to work.

3

Boring wasn't a big enough word to describe the comments from last year's crop of editors. I did two laps around the room wondering if this was a missed form of torture. Maybe I could get a job abroad and lobby to have this on the Geneva Convention's prohibition list.

After a third lap, I sat. The next up was from Ted Strohmeyer. Normally, I'd have tossed that on the rejection pile faster than a Boy Scout could throw kindling on a fire. But Tom had asked one favor I couldn't grant. Maybe I could give him another. I pulled Strohmeyer's typed sixty-page submission toward me and started to read.

Ten minutes later, I stood up, stunned. It was good, really good. Maybe there were some brains back there behind all the family money and testosterone I'd seen on display. I mean, his father could pull a lot of strings, but take the LSAT for the kid wasn't one of them. Perhaps old Ted had some smarts in him after all.

Reenergized, I picked up the note. Public schools was the subject. Not intellectual property or securities law, the topics my classmates saw as the ticket to a great job. He had picked something that could really make a difference to real people, the kind of people who didn't have access to top flight lawyers.

Strohmeyer had written about inequities in public schools. Cleveland and Cuyahoga County probably had some of the most unequal in the country. Schools from suburbs like Rocky River and Shaker Heights could run circles around the schools in Cleveland neighborhoods. My parents had sacrificed a lot to send me to Catholic school from first grade through St. Joseph High School. Education had been too important in my family to leave it up to the whim of politicians and bureaucratic administrators. Other kids, I knew, weren't so lucky.

Strohmeyer had devised a method that states, counties, or cities could use to eliminate the problem of poor versus rich school districts. It was such a good idea, I could only hope our publication of the comment would launch a nationwide discussion on how to make schools better for everyone. After I turned the last page of the submission, I finally—guiltily—looked at the clock again. It was four.

Damn, there was no way I could make it at the promised time.

I picked up the phone. "Mama," I said into the receiver. "I'll be there about six. Is that okay?"

"Lieb, you okay? You with Tom?"

I wanted to lie and tell her yes, my soon-to-be fiancé was the one keeping me from Good Friday dinner. She'd accept that excuse without blinking an eyelash.

"No, Mama, just some work. I'll leave as soon as I'm done," I said.

My mother's disapproval came through the phone like a tidal wave. Spending time with 'Catholic boys going somewhere' had always been good. Working hard so I could secure my own future, had always been suspect in my mother's eyes. Even though I'd of course tell her about my engagement minutes after it happened, I still caught her perusing the Sunday Celebrations section like my engagement photo would surprise her one weekend morning.

"Whatever you have to do, dear," she said. "Be sure to wish Tom a happy Easter before you come home."

As if Tom were here. He'd been assured a job in county or state government from the minute he'd stepped through the door first year. He'd never done more than he had to, to get by. Neither his dad, nor uncle or one of their minions would be scrutinizing his transcripts for a mediocre performance.

After agreeing to pass along her well wishes, and hanging up the phone, I turned to the LexisNexis computer terminal the legal research company had installed in the room. Lexis and Westlaw gave law students free machines and free searches hoping we'd sign up to be customers for life of their uber expensive proprietary services.

I was glad to be going to a law firm with clients with deep enough pockets to pay for research. Some of my classmates who were unemployed and talking about hanging out their own shingle would have a hell of a time figuring out how to get their hands on the latest research at a cut-rate price.

I shook my head of the worries of my less fortunate class-mates. I was sure it would work out for them. Turning back to Strohmeyer's note, I had to marvel. It was good. It would definitely be published as long as someone else hadn't pub-lished something just like it recently. Everyone wanted to be on the cutting edge of legal research, but so few were. I did not want to oversee publication of something that was the second or third article on a topic. It would only cement our status as a second rate school behind Ohio State and Case Western Reserve.

My fingers flew over the keys, typing in a search about disestablishing local school districts and reorganizing them in different regional configurations. If law school had been good for one thing it had been teaching me super quick ways to find the information I needed.

I stared at the black and white words on the monitor in disbelief.

Crap.

What I'd found wasn't good.

At all.

The results scrolling on the screen pricked my balloon of anticipation and released air. There were two other law re-view articles on the topic. Which would have been fine, but one had been published only a year ago. I printed them both anyway, hoping against hope I could find a way to salvage Strohmeyer's work.

"I was hoping you were here," a voice said, scaring the shit out of me.

Tom.

Papers flew from my hand, landing in warm toner scented piles.

"My mom wishes you a happy Easter," I said dutifully as I gathered the scattered papers from the floor near the printer.

"Didn't mean to scare you. Was out for a couple of beers with Sullivan and the guys. Knew you'd be here."

"It's Good Friday."

"And you're a good girl, who does good work. Good girls stay late at school."

"Are you drunk?" Tom wasn't usually so glib.

"Not too drunk to know I've been neglecting you." Quick as lightning, Tom went from the tiny office's front door to banding his arms around me. A sloppy kiss grazed my cheek. "We should lock that door," Tom said while his hand made its way to my breast.

"Tom, stop," I said, pushing him away. I loved him. I wanted him. I wanted him to want me. But not like this.

"We're young. We're in love. I think we should act like it."

"Act? Why is it so hard for you want me? Am I that repulsive?" I nearly shrunk away in shame. I had no idea what had possessed me to ask the one thing I feared to be true.

Tom let go of me. Sat hard in Erwin Gesick's chair.

"Catholic guilt, Casey. How many times did the priest at your parish tell you not to have sex before marriage? Because Father Hughes seems to say it every time I'm within spitting distance of the church. The older I get, the more I hear it.

"We've already had sex before marriage, Tom," I pointed out. I didn't point out that it hadn't been very often nor satisfying. My own Catholic guilt kept me quiet on that account. "I don't think the sin gets any worse the fifth time or the fiftieth."

"Fuck me. I'm sloshed." He laid his head on his hands, turned his face toward me. "What are you beavering away at on Good Friday?"

"Trying to do you a favor."

"How's that?" He tried to wrinkle his brow in question, but I think that the alcohol had relaxed him too much to have perfect control over his face.

"Gotta pick a student comment for publication. I was going to pick Ted Strohmeyer's."

"Really? That's a girl having my back. Love you for that." I let the validation wash over me before I let Tom down.

"I don't think it will fly, though."

"Why?"

"Same topic a Professor..." I sorted through the stack until I found the top sheet from the printer. "...Richard Holloman wrote about a year ago."

"What journal?"

"Valparaiso?" I stumbled through the pronunciation. I scrutinized the tiny print further. "School in Indiana."

"You said a year ago?" I nodded. "When would this come out?"

"Next fall."

"So by then, we're talking eighteen months. Like two or three years between one paper and the next."

"What are you saying?"

"That you do the Brodys and Ed Strohmeyer a solid. You could publish it. We'd really appreciate it, and who would say anything anyway? You think the managing partner of the Cleveland office of Morrell Gates is going to call you in and chastise you for not publishing a completely one-of-a-kind original comment?"

Against my better nature, I wavered a little. "Sit tight. Let me have a quick look to make sure they're not too similar and then, sure, why not?"

Tom pulled my hand to his lips. The kiss he placed there was the sweetest gesture he'd made in a while. My stomach squeezed a little. All sorts of hope about our future together blossomed.

He kicked back in Gesick's chair, propping his shoes on the editor-in-chief's desk.

I pulled Holloman's article toward me and started reading. Five seconds later I stopped. I fished through the stacks on my desk and retrieved Strohmeyer's submission. I highlighted first Holloman's words, then Strohmeyer's.

Fucking A.

He'd copied the damned article nearly word for word. While Tom dozed, I used a pink pen to highlight Holloman's article, and a yellow for Strohmeyers. When I was done, it looked like a unicorn had bled all over the papers, minus the glitter.

I kicked Gesick's chair. "Tom," I said.

My boyfriend's chocolate brown eyes snapped open. "What? You ready to go? We should go back to your place. Halfway sober, I can—"

"It's Good Friday," I said, trying to hide my exasperation. Where had this Tom been when I was parading around in stupid lingerie I could scarcely afford, my hands down his pants trying to get him in the mood? "I have to go to West Boulevard tonight."

"Oh, later then?"

Because of course I was going to bail on a fish dinner for sex. My mom loved Tom, but not that much. I pushed thoughts of fish, fowl, and the bedroom aside.

"I've got to show you something."

Tom knew serious when he heard it. He sat up in the chair looking surprisingly like an adult.

"What? Are you going to be able to publish Strohmeyer?"

"No. Definitely, no." I extended the two stacks of paper toward him. "Have a look at this."

Tom flipped through the stacks, barely looking at the words. "What in the hell is all this?"

"Look here," I pointed to the first page. "Professor Holloman wrote, 'The school funding dilemma plagues cities, counties, and municipal districts across the United States."

Shifting the papers, I pointed to the exact same passage in Strohmeyers comment.

"Okay. That's not the most original sentence ever. If you asked me, I'm sure I'd say school funding is a dilemma that plagues cities."

"Fine." I flipped thirty pages until I found another passage, I'd labeled as number fifty-two. "Nineteen states, included two of the most populous, Florida and California, fail to provide sufficient funding to address the needs of students in the states' numerous high poverty districts, despite high concentrations of such districts within their borders."

I pointed to the same passage on page thirty-seven of Holloman's work.

"I see the problem. So don't publish it. You were doing it as a favor to me anyway. This is why Ted needs your help. See the kind of trouble he gets in when he tries to do this all on his own."

"My help? He doesn't need my help. He needs a conscience."

"Casey. Whoa there. Slow down. It's not like he's some gang banger killing people in cold blood. So he couldn't figure this out on his own, so he borrowed the words of some professor. You'll bury it. It'll never see the light of day. No harm. No foul."

"What about the law school's code of ethics?"

Tom used his right hand to shift the too-long blond mop that sometimes fell in his face, away from his eyes. Despite the removal of the Dennis the Menace hair obscuring his eyes, he squinted at me.

"What about it?"

I pulled the law school handbook from the shelf above my desk that held a couple of Black's Law Dictionaries and the latest edition of the Bluebook.

"Plagiarizing, or representing someone else's written work as one's own without acknowledgment or with insufficient, or improper acknowledgment is a violation of the Code of Academic Integrity."

"That's a lot of words that don't say much. I haven't been to training yet for the Prosecuting Attorney's office, but I'm going to hazard a guess that a violation of the Code of…what in the hell was it again?"

"Academic Integrity."

"Whatever, doesn't rise to the level of an indictable offense."

I thumbed the pages of the book I'd read more than once. I always figured a school with a job of teaching future lawyers should have rules and abide by them.

"They have all sorts of reporting requirements and procedures in here."

"You're forgetting one thing, Casey."

"What?"

"Ted graduated some ten months ago. He's no longer subject to whatever dummy procedures the school could dream up."

"You have a point there. But I think I should take these to the dean nonetheless."

"Dean Condit?"

"That's what it says here. All reports of misrepresentation of another's work as one's own shall be reported to the Dean's office when discovered."

"Look, you're not going to do the Strohmeyers a favor. I get that. Trust me, I get that. I'm sorry to have asked you, and I'll let my dad and his dad Ed know that's a total no go. And I'll tell them why. But beyond that, don't waste your time. You have, what, a couple more weeks doing this crap. You'll graduate, and we can spend the summer studying for the bar and planning out our lives."

"So should I just bin all this?" I gestured to the stacks of highlighted papers.

"There's a blue recycling can in the corner. How 'bout I drive you to West Avenue, say hi to your mom and dad, before I get back to Lakewood?"

"I don't know…"

"Ted fucked up. You didn't. Let all this go. I was wondering if you're thinking of getting a bigger apartment this summer?"

"Why?" I tried not to get whiplash from the change of subject. Making neat stacks of papers, I thought about his question. My nine hundred square foot apartment in Shaker Square was just fine. It had become home over the last three years.

"My mom has a little house on Summit Avenue that she's fixed up."

"Summit? Isn't that right near the water?" I think I'd made a wrong turn near the street on one of the few occasions I'd been invited to the Brody mansion in Lakewood.

"We should see it this weekend. Maybe you can slip away from your family and mass for a few minutes."

"Maybe I can skip mass this year altogether." God would want me married, and if I had to skip one day of church to move that process forward, I was willing to risk my immortal soul.

4

Missing Easter Sunday mass had been non-negotiable. My mother had, she said, put a lot of time and effort into the protection of my eternal soul, and she wasn't risking it, even for Tom. So I'd had to tell him to push off the viewing. I hadn't heard from him much during the spring recess week. I'd mostly spent the week working with the second-years refining their comments and pondering my responsibility to the school vis-à-vis Ted Strohmeyer. I wasn't quite convinced that doing nothing was best.

"You're home," Tom said in greeting when I picked up the ringing telephone.

"Trying to relax a little on the last day before it gets intense. Only two more weeks of class before law school is over. I can't quite believe that I made it."

"Almost all of us did," Tom said.

There had been the usual dropouts, mostly part-timers, but the rest of us had stuck it out even when it had been hard.

"What's up?" I asked, looking around my apartment. It was clean. My laundry was done. If Tom wanted to come over, I was more than game, but I didn't want to be the one to ask. I was starting to think I'd done altogether too much asking over the years.

"Got the keys to Summit."

Excited about the future, I took down the address and directions and practically ran down the four flights to my car, risking not only my immortal soul, but my heart as well. Maybe I'd take Morrell Gates up on that free gym membership.

Half an hour of leg jiggling and steering wheel tapping later, I pulled my Honda up to the metal barrier on the dead end street. As soon as I started work, I'd get a new car. I looked around at the driveways in the neighborhood. The Subaru Forester I had my eye on, would fit right in. Putting my slightly dented car into park, I peered out at the lake. Whitecaps whipped up on Lake Erie. The sound of another car had me flicking my eyes toward the rearview mirror. Tom's sleek little Acura roared into the driveway of the Summit Avenue house.

Pulling my scarf tight, I pushed open my car door. The wind made the job harder than normal.

"Great location," I shouted over the wind.

"C'mon in," Tom called. The turned up collar of his pea coat was his only nod to the chilly spring weather.

I followed him down a path to the front or side of the house, I couldn't quite tell.

"It's a flag lot," Tom said, answering my unasked question.

"Got it." There were a few of these in Cleveland. Lots that had narrow entrances, leading to otherwise square plots. On Summit, it meant that two houses could have waterfront land without any pesky street ruining the views.

My boyfriend produced a large key ring. After trial and error, he located one that opened the dead bolt.

The smell of fresh paint was what I noticed first. Tom dropped the keys on the arms of a beautiful leather couch.

"Who lives here?" It was fully furnished in a décor I'd call confirmed bachelor. From where I was standing, there was only leather and wood. I half expected someone my dad's age to shuffle into the room, plaid robe firmly belted, carrying bourbon and a pipe.

"One of my uncles was...taking a break from...he was using it." Tom stumbled through the explanation that did little to conceal family dysfunction.

"And he's not now?" I gestured to the furniture and rugs that remained.

"It needed a bunch of work. He had it done while he was here. Now my mom's thinking we could have it."

"Furnished?" Wood and leather could grow on me.

"It's all ours. All we have to do is say yes. We could move in on June first."

The house wasn't small. It was the only single-story ranch I'd ever seen in Lakewood, but that only meant it was probably fifteen hundred square feet instead of three thousand.

I spun around on my sneakered foot, fantasies of the future rolling around in my head. I could see myself studying for the bar while sitting on the deck I could see from the three-season porch off the open living room and kitchen. We could have coffee and strudel at the stone counters. I could wash dishes while watching tall ships come and go on the lake.

"When was this built?" I said, rubbing my hand along the stained wood around the fireplace.

"Don't know. Long time ago like your apartment. It's perfect for us, right? You like all the old stuff, molding, wood floors and all that jazz. But I like new, and this has it. The kitchen, bathrooms, everything was redone."

When he didn't drop on bended knee, I asked for a tour instead. Even though the house was a single story, it was laid out so that nearly every room had a view of the lake. The kitchen was done in dark cabinets and stone counters. The bathrooms were immaculate in white tile and marble.

"This is amazing," I said because it was. "How far is the drive downtown?" In the bedroom where we were standing, I pointed east.

"Twenty minutes easy."

Tom uncharacteristically grabbed my hand and pulled me toward him.

"Say yes. Let's do this. Take the next step with me."

"Tom..." I pulled away. I plopped down on the four poster bed in what I guessed was the master, and stared at the gray and white water. The window was a replica of the one in the living room. It was large, rectangular, and horizontal, designed to frame the view. I took in everything like it was a movie, and I was the heroine.

"Are you serious about this?" I asked.

Tom was practically giving me the keys to the kingdom. I couldn't say what was making me uneasy.

"What do I have to do to convince you?" he asked, sitting next to me. His large hand rested on my denim-clad thigh.

I wanted to say, put a ring on my finger, make it official. Instead, I relented. "I don't need any convincing. I'm in!"

Gently Tom lay me down on the bed, his thigh levering over mine. "You've made me a very happy man."

Then he kissed me. Ten minutes later, we were making use of the four-poster bed in the room with the lake view that gave the feeling of the utmost in privacy. My heart thudded in anticipation of all that was coming now and in the future.

5

"This came for you," Gesick said, tossing a thick ivory envelope on my desk.

"What's this?"

"Looks like a wedding invitation. You better open it."

It wasn't an invitation to my own wedding—that was for sure. Maybe I'd have something like this next spring. I turned over the card in my hands. Embossed silver font made the return address nearly unreadable. I rubbed my hands over the letters like a blind person reading Braille. Morrell Gates. Leaning forward in my chair, I grabbed for a letter opener I'd gotten as a prize for one moot court competition or another.

I slipped the heavy brass along the top seam. The card inside was even heavier stock than the envelope. With effort, I eased it out. The invitation requested the honor of my presence at a reception immediately following commencement on the nineteenth of May. I scanned the address. Fancy. The shindig would be hosted at the Wyndham hotel in Playhouse Square.

Erwin Gesick left his chair and leaned over my shoulder. "So what is it?"

"Post commencement reception for new associates," I said, handing the invitation to him. I fished inside the envelope and found the RSVP card. Without hesitation, I plucked the first pen I saw and ticked the box that said I was going. For the number of guests, I hesitated.

"I'd happily go as your date," Gesick said as my hand hovered over the card.

"Would you now? I don't think Tom would like to share."

"Do you like to share?" His question grumbled low in his chest.

"Tom and I are moving in together after graduation," I blurted out. Five seconds later, I was embarrassed that I felt the need to justify my relationship with Gesick.

"Getting married, then?"

"Eventually, Erwin. Right now I'm going to add three guests to this for my mom, dad, and Tom."

He tossed the invitation on my desk. "What's all this highlighting you've got going on here?"

Strohmeyer. I hadn't taken the stuff home, nor had I recycled it like Tom had suggested.

"Stuff I'm working on."

"We're done here, Casey. You know that, right? Two more weeks of class, exams, then graduation. There isn't a thing more we have to do except plan a bar trip."

I gathered up the papers, collated and stacked them. "Just wanted to leave everything in tip top shape for the next crew. When are elections, anyway?"

"They'll be at the next editor's meeting. We'll have everyone in on that, not just us. Gotta prepare the next generation for their work. Hopefully there will be eager beavers like you dying to take over before May."

Knuckles rapped on the door. Gesick moved away to unlock it. Never was I so thankful to see Tom. I didn't quite know how to continue to rebuff Gesick's less than subtle come-ons. With Tom here, he didn't dare insinuate anything about dinner or dates in Canton.

"Got a surprise," Tom said. He held up a fat envelope in his hand.

"I like surprises," I said. Actually, I hated surprises. People always wanted you to be happy. I never knew how to react. Like yesterday with the house. Even though I loved the idea of moving in with Tom, I'd have preferred a discussion of it rather than a fait accompli.

"Good." He handed me my second mystery envelope of the day.

The nondescript blue and green paper was slippery in my hands. I lifted the flap. Dot matrix printed pages stared back at me. I closed my eyes to clear my head and looked at it again. CLE, DUB, and SXF initials jumped out. I slipped the thick sheaf of papers out.

"Are these tickets?"

"My graduation gift to you."

"Where is SXF?" I stumbled over the tongue-twisting initials.

"Berlin," Gesick said. I looked over at the editor-in-chief. "As in Germany."

"He's right. First class tickets to Dublin and Berlin. I figured we'd spend a week in the country where my family is from and another in yours."

"I...don't have a passport," I said.

"We leave on August first, right after the bar exam. If you apply now, you'll have it in time."

"Wow. This is so...I don't know what to say..."

"Thanks. I love you, would be enough."

Gesick's eye roll didn't go unnoticed.

"Thanks, I love you!" I said, and then jumped up to throw my arms around his neck.

Tom disentangled me and looked at his watch. "Gotta get to my Capital Punishment seminar. I'll take these for safekeeping. Make sure you go to the post office and apply for your passport."

Like a whirlwind, Tom was gone as quickly as he'd come.

"You're tying your fate to Tom Brody?" Gesick asked. The thinly veiled veneer of politeness he usually had was gone. His disgust with Tom was on full display.

"Erwin. Look, you said yourself, we've only got weeks left, okay? You've been making all kinds of snide remarks about Tom. If you have something you want to say, do it now, or stop. I'm with him, and unless you tell me he's a serial killer, or child molester..." I gestured between the closed door and myself. "He and I being a couple won't change. Not today, tomorrow, or six months from now."

"So you're throwing down the gauntlet, 'eh?"

"Lulu's out there waiting for me. I can see her sparkling from here. In ten minutes, I have Transnational Litigation. Go."

Gesick stood and went to open the door. He waved in my best friend.

"What? I don't do law review." Lulu looked around the small office as though we were a contagious disease incubator.

"You should hear this."

Lulu looked at me, her face a question. I shrugged. We both turned to Gesick.

"Do you remember the trip to Las Vegas some of the guys took for Levy Berg's bachelor party?"

"In the spring of first year?" I asked, trying to remember back that far. During that spring, I'd barely recovered from the shock of my first semester of law school or the fact that I was near the top of my class. Who went where hadn't been on my radar.

Lulu squinted her eyes behind the glasses. "It was Tom, Jason Sullivan, Strohmeyer, and who all knows who else," she answered. Lulu had always been a keener observer than I.

"Me," Gesick said, thumping his chest. "Berg and I lived on the same floor first year."

"Clock's ticking," I said, tapping my watch deliberately. "I don't have time for a trip down memory lane."

"So we're respectable guys. On the plane out, we'd talked about drinking, maybe hitting up a club or two. Your boyfriend pulled a list of strip clubs out of his carryon bag."

I worked to keep a carefully blank expression on my face. For all the time we'd been together, Tom had claimed to have a lower than average sex drive, or be stressed out, or...or whatever. He'd always had some excuse as to why he wasn't much interested in sex. This story, if it were true, was like a kick in the gut.

"So, what? Casey is supposed to be mad at Tom for liking to look? Every red-blooded male I've ever met—straight or gay—likes to look," Lulu said.

"Tom went a step further than looking. He ordered a pair of strippers to come up to Berg's suite. After the dancing, Tom disappeared to a bedroom with one of them."

"Did you watch? Cause otherwise we're about to jump into a whole lot of speculation."

"No, Lulu, I didn't watch. But I'm not deaf. They weren't briefing property cases in there."

"That's it, Erwin?" I asked shaking my head in disgust. "You've been making snide remarks for a year over something that happened in Vegas in nineteen ninety four?"

"He cheated on you. You'd only been going out for about two months, and there he was shacking up with some random woman, when he had you at home."

"While I appreciate your concern, Tom and my relationship is private. It's been good working with you on law review these last couple of years, but this, whatever relationship there is between us, will never been more than friends. Okay? We've gotta go."

I grabbed my best friend's backpack and hauled ass from the room.

6

"So what do you think of the EU court of arbitration cases? Do you think it will ever come up? I think most of Dalton Lacey's cases still involve manufactured goods." Lulu stopped speaking to me only long enough to place our lunch orders. They weren't any different today than they'd been the week before or the week before that. She had pumpkin with black bean sauce, hold the rice. I had chow fun with everything.

I watched the waitress walk to the back in shoes that looked like they'd be hell before the end of the day.

Lulu's fingers snapped in front of me.

"Hello in there. You didn't answer the question."

"Do you honestly think I heard a thing Professor Sinclair said today? Erwin Gesick's words were too busy bouncing around in my head," I admitted.

"Oh, Casey. You were so cool in there, I didn't think it bothered you. You talked about the new Lakewood house all the way to class."

"How in the hell could it not...bother me? I think I remember that stupid bachelor party being in February or something. We started going out, more or less exclusively, right after Christmas."

"Do you think it's true? Gesick's had a thing for you forever. I think he's just pissed you picked Tom over him."

"Picked Tom over him? Erwin was never in the running. He's not even my type."

"He's had a crush on you a mile wide."

"I don't want any part of a guy like that. He bullies. He's mean. He likes to cut corners." I held up a hand when Lulu's mouth started to open. "Don't give me that shit about he's mean because he likes you. That works in kindergarten. After that, it's misogyny.

Lulu pursed her lips, hard, but thought better of speaking.

I was grateful we were off Gesick. I'd always been a little nervous that he was going to do something to me, but with a month or so left, I was happy to close the door on the possibility of spending any more time with him than was necessary.

"Are you going to talk to Tom about it?" she asked. "The stripper thing?"

"Hell, no. We're moving in together in June. He bought us bar trip tickets for August. Maybe he wasn't committed then. But now he's one hundred percent in. Dredging up the past would be beyond stupid."

Our food came, and I dug into my noodles like I hadn't eaten in weeks.

"Are they that good?" she asked as she watched me inhale.

"No, Lulu," I pushed the plate to the side. "This Tom and Erwin Gesick crap doesn't even really matter. I've got a much bigger problem on my hands."

Gesick and Tom were replaced by Strohmeyer and like that, my appetite disappeared.

"What? From where I'm sitting, things are looking mighty fine for you."

I fished in my bag and pulled out the stacks of documents. Shoving them over to Lulu, I said, "Ted Strohmeyer submitted a completely plagiarized comment."

"Oh, my god!" She gasped so loudly, the family that owned the restaurant looked up from their hasty lunch in a corner booth. When one of them started to rise, Lulu waved them away then fell into laughter. "That's so not a shock. Is there anything that guy didn't do to flout rules? They do say that the rules are different for the rich." And like that, she went back to her pumpkin and black bean sauce.

"But they shouldn't be." I was emphatic. "Fair should be fair. Some people shouldn't get to cut corners while other people have to work their asses off."

"What about Tom? There's been a hiring freeze at the prosecutor's office since the last recession, but they found a place for him. That's bending the rules for sure."

Called on my duplicity, I shifted in my seat. "Look, what Tom did was nepotism, not illegal, at least in county government. They're not the Kennedys. What Ted did was a clear violation of the school rules."

"So what are you going to do?"

"The handbook and code of ethics says I need to turn it over to the dean."

"Then what?"

"I don't know. But then it's out of my hands. At no point do I want it getting back to me that I somehow had a hand in helping Ted Strohmeyer cheat. I mean, if I cover it up, bury it, isn't that what I'm doing? Being complicit?" How many politicians had I watched implode in the pages of the Plain Dealer as they claimed not to know what was going on in their own office or department?

"What does Tom say?"

"Not much. But he's no longer asking me to 'help' out Ted at Morrell Gates."

"So there's an upside to all this."

"I guess," I said, then pushed away from the table. I normally loved our post class Chinese meals, but I'd lost my appetite for this one. Too much going on to enjoy the food today, I guessed.

"Where you going? You usually finish off your noodles."

I heaved the stack back into my bag. "Going to Dean Condit's office. I need to make this someone else's problem. Also, I should go and use the law review copier while I still can. Going to make one of those flyers with the little strips."

"For what?"

"Sublet my place in Shaker Square. Someone around here who's registered for summer classes probably has a nine-month lease that's running out. They can have my place and I don't have to eat the rent for June, July and August."

"You're moving in, huh? It's all done except the wedding."

"No reason not to. If we're going to get married, we're going to live together someday. Might as well get a jump on the situation. Plus I really don't have any more money to lay out. I've spent all the cash I earned last summer. Won't see my first big paycheck until September. I can't expect Tom to float me completely."

"Mind if I take your food home?" Lulu asked, her eyes not quite meeting mine.

"Go ahead. Between law review get-togethers and Morrell Gates, I think I have food covered for the next few weeks."

I left Lulu munching vegetables and flipping through the red and black Transnational Law casebook. If we judged legal textbooks by their covers, the conclusion would be boring and dry as dust. Turning back toward the school, I lifted my umbrella against the spatter of rain and walked as quickly as I could. I'd blown out my hair before school. I was starting to think I liked it straight.

Once at school, I made my way to the Dean's office. The funeral parlor quiet interior and plush carpet was a world away from what we students had in our offices.

"How can I help you?" an efficient assistant asked me long before I'd had a chance to drop my umbrella in the stand by the door. It was clear that nary a drop of water landed on these office floors if she could help it.

"I need to see Dean Condit. It's important."

"Do you have an appointment?" Her voice was as smooth as the butter my mother spread in between the layers of strudel.

"No. It's about a violation of the code of ethics." I rooted around in my bag and found the highlighted stacks of pages then held them out.

"Oh, okay." She looked from me to the papers in my hand and back. The thick stack of papers had her up and out of her chair. "Let me run in and see if the dean has a few minutes."

Before I could scope out a comfortable chair, the secretary was back in a flash. "The dean can see you now."

She led me to the inner sanctum of the dean's office. I'd only been there twice, once when I'd been among the students with the highest grades first year, and the other time when I'd been elected Senior Comment Editor. Both occasions had involved a lot of handshaking and head nodding on my part. I'd never said more than a few words or initiated a discussion with the dean.

"Good morning, Ms. Cort. Della says you have something you want to discuss."

I sat in the chair nearest his desk without an express invitation because I didn't think my nervous legs could hold me much longer.

"I'm Senior Comment Editor for the law review," I prefaced.

"Yes I'm aware," Dean Condit said, his smile rueful.

"Well, I was doing some cleanup, reviewing comments for publication in next year's fall issue, and I was considering one for publication."

"Yes, and..."

"Well, when I went to look for similar publications on the subject, because, well you know, law reviews should cover novel areas of law, I found that the submitted comment lifted entire passages from a publication from a Professor Holloman in a Valparaiso article."

"I'm familiar with Professor Holloman. He does some excellent research in areas of education law and funding. What you are saying is quite concerning. We take ethics and honor code violations very seriously here."

Relief flooded through me. My stomach knots untied. I knew I'd been right to be concerned. I leaned forward and placed the sheaf of papers on Dean Condit's blotter.

"The student is Ted Strohmeyer?" The dean asked, looking up at me, his brow heavily furrowed.

"Yes, I..." I didn't say anymore. What could I say to explain why someone so privileged would bother stooping to plagiarism when he didn't need to do it to graduate, or get a job, or achieve anything, really.

"Thanks, Ms. Cort. I'll consult with the law review faculty liaison, Professor Haynes. We'll take the matter under advisement."

"Oh, okay. Um, well, thanks for making the time to see me," I said. It hadn't been the outrage I'd expected. But as I gathered my bag, raincoat, and umbrella, I quickly realized that as dean, he probably came across stuff like this every day. He'd probably chucked outrage out the door after the first year on the job.

"Good luck with the bar and your job at Morrell Gates."

"Thanks, I'm looking forward to what comes next." I took my leave.

I nodded to Della on the way out. I sort of wanted to leave contact information or something, but they didn't need that from me. No doubt they had a database a mile wide with information for each and every one of us. If not for use now, then for later when hitting us up for alumni donations, their primary reason for keeping in contact.

I went back to the law review office I shared with Gesick, thanking my lucky stars it was empty. I sat down at the computer and typed out a sublet ad for my apartment, then printed it. After foraging for scissors, I made the tiny little cuts I'd seen in so many ads during my years at undergrad and then here.

Attaching tiny pieces of tape to the unruffled edges of the eight by ten pages made my eyes well up. The future was looking so different from the past. My cute little first apartment, I'd miss it. It was the first real place I'd ever had on my own, but the coming months and years were looking even brighter than the present. I'd always carry nostalgia for Shaker Square, though.

The door jerked in my hand as I pulled it open to leave. Gesick. I swear the man was suddenly everywhere.

"What's that?" he asked and pointed to my flyers.

"Need a sublet?" I said, tearing off a tiny strip with my name and phone number and pushing it into his hand.

"Nope, Casey I don't." The familiar, friendly tone he'd been using the last couple of days was gone. Even the patronizing tone he saved for dressing me down in meetings was nowhere in sight.

"Oh, okay, then," I said, ready to get this up on the community bulletin board next to the student mailboxes.

"Not so fast," Gesick said, his sudden grip around my wrist firm. He pulled me back into the office, slamming the door behind us.

I'd never been afraid of being in an office with him. Never really been afraid of any man, but Gesick's sudden change in behavior kind of had me wishing I'd gone with

Lulu to the self defense classes she'd taken first year when we all stayed late with our study groups, navigating cold, dark parking lots well after hours.

"What the fuck, Erwin! I'm with Tom. I'm not going to kiss you, date you, or visit you in Canton. Locking me in a room with you won't change that."

"This is not about some stupid hookup, Casey. I just came down here from Dean Condit's office."

Even though I hadn't put a foot wrong in my entire three years of law school, panic flooded my veins, speeding my heart to attack levels. My brain emptied of all its words. I couldn't think of anything to say, so I stood mute.

Gesick leaned toward me. "You were there...today... perhaps you remember turning in a comment about Ted Strohmeyer and accusing him of plagiarism."

Adrenaline left as quickly as it had come, leaving me shaky. I dropped my stuff on my desk and sat heavily in my chair.

"The handbook requires reporting," I said, knowing it sounded lame, a tattletale's excuse.

"You didn't think to run it up the chain of command?"

"We're not the military," I retorted. Chain of command my ass.

"And you're not editor-in-chief." Gesick's voice was tight with fury. Misplaced fury, if you asked me.

"Well, it's done. It was the right thing to do." I prided myself on always doing the right thing. The Catholic Church was less than perfect, but I'd learned the importance of telling the truth from the nuns and Jesuit priests who'd had a heavy hand in my moral upbringing.

"Was it?"

"Why wouldn't it be?"

"We could have handled it internally."

"I did handle it internally. It's not like I went to the Plain Dealer or something."

"By not publishing it is how we should have handled it," Gesick said with controlled fury. "By sending the author a letter noting our plan to take it out of consideration."

"That's like sending a thief a letter asking him not to steal anymore."

"Maybe you should ask your boyfriend about the penal codes. We're not judge, jury, and executioner. We're here to publish articles and comments. That's all."

"So then maybe the dean won't do anything. I don't know. I just didn't want the responsibility to make any kind of decision."

"Do nothing. The dean can't 'do nothing.' You've put a ticking time bomb in his hands. The scion of one of the most prominent families in Cleveland has done a naughty thing. If he 'does nothing' then it will come back to bite him in the ass. Maybe not today. Maybe not tomorrow. But sometime. If he takes it to the Judicial Board, then what, a bunch of students and faculty sit around thinking up ways to censure someone who's already graduated, doing nothing more than embarrassing the law school in the process because of course last year's Senior Comment Editor should have noticed something as obvious as plagiarism."

I wasn't going to let him guilt me. I knew in my heart I'd done the right thing, passing the buck. If anything blew up, I wanted to be well out of blast range.

"This is Dean Condit's job, Erwin. He gets paid in dollars. I get paid in paper cuts. I'm one hundred percent sure I've done the right thing."

Either way it wasn't my problem anymore. I hadn't been Strohmeyer's editor. I hadn't plagiarized.

"I'm outta here. I don't have anything on deck until Wednesday."

I didn't bother with good-bye. I posted my flyers then took myself home through the rain without the umbrella. To hell with the hair.

7

"Lieb, it's so good to have you home." My mother embraced me in a warm cinnamon-scented hug.

"What are you baking?" I asked, looking at the traces of flour and pastry on her apron.

"Franzbrötchen."

"I love those. It's been a long time since I've had any." So many mornings my mom had filled the kitchen with the scent of the German cinnamon rolls.

"I wanted to celebrate you moving back in."

"Mom. You know it's not permanent. The guy who wanted to sublet my place had a problem with his room- mate and asked to move in early."

"I'm just glad to have my baby home. What do you need help with?"

"My clothes are in the car. Just some spring stuff. The heavy winter sweaters and coats I'll get from Shaker Square and take them directly to Summit."

"Let your dad get that," my mother said then turned back toward the kitchen.

Summit. I'd been pretty careful not to bring it up over the last couple of weeks, but I'd walked right into it not five seconds in the house. I made a vow to myself to be a lot more careful over the next month.

I followed her into the kitchen. The croissant shaped cinnamon rolls were on a baking sheet, all puffed and ready to go into the oven.

"I'll be studying a lot over the next week or so, Mama. So I won't really be bothering you."

"Oh, you being here is no bother at all. None at all." My mom walked toward the back of the kitchen and called out the back window, "Peter! Come help Casey."

My dad came in from the backyard. I had no idea what he was doing back there. It didn't seem warm enough for planting vegetables, but I didn't ask. He kissed me on the top of my head. I looked up at him. His curly hair was a bit grayer and a bit thinner than last time. "Good to see you. What's in the car?"

"Just a suitcase and my overnight bag. Going to be studying in my sweats, so not too heavy."

"I'll get it for you and put everything in your room. Keep your mother company a bit." My dad left through the front of the house.

My mom dusted her hands on an apron covered with preening hens and roosters. Heat filled the room when my mother heaved open the oven door and popped in the trays of rolls. The white enameled stove would have been at home in the pioneer era. Whenever I'd asked if she wanted something new, sleek, and modern like we'd see in the Sunday newspaper flyers, my mother had always said no, she wanted to keep one that reminded her of the old days.

"Do you want me to set the timer for you?" I asked.

"Oh, did I forget? No need. It's all up here. Speaking of memory, let me see…" My mother stood stock still for a moment, then lifted a stack of envelopes from the kitchen counter. She handed it all to me.

Ah, my mail. I'd been kind of lax about changing my address. Utility bills came to me at my North Moreland address, but the rest, car insurance, school stuff, all of it was still delivered to West Boulevard. As I shuffled through the stack and weeded out the junk, I made a mental note to change my address to Summit at the same time I applied for a passport.

"This is it?" I asked. The stack minus catalogs was woefully thin.

"Let me…" Mama took out the browned rolls. My mouth watered in anticipation.

"Casey, can you put these on cooling racks? I need to find the other thing that came for you."

I fished a spatula from a cabinet drawer and moved all but two rolls to the racks my mom had set up on the counter. The remaining, I put on a plate for myself. They were best hot.

"Everything's upstairs. I moved your car as well," my father said, stepping back into the kitchen.

"Thanks, Daddy. You want a roll?"

"Somehow I don't think this is what the doctor meant by low-fat, low-sugar foods."

"Is there something wrong?" I asked, trying to keep the panic from my voice.

"Just age," he said, waving away my question. "Pass me a roll. It won't kill me."

I got two more plates from the shelf and put a roll on each. My mother would say she didn't want one, shouldn't eat one, then would finally relent. Maybe if I put the roll on the plate, I could skip that conversation for the day.

"What did you do? The postman made me sign for this." My mother came into the room with a white business envelope, its top visibly separated.

"Ma, I've asked you to stop opening my mail. As an adult I need privacy."

As if I hadn't spoken, or grown up past ten, my mother pulled a letter from the envelope. "Says here you've been summoned to a hearing before some review board."

I sighed. Ted Strohmeyer. I guess it wasn't just going to go away.

"I didn't want to get into it," I said to my parents. "But I guess I should tell you that I had to report plagiarism to the dean of the law school."

"What happened?" my father asked.

"Ted Strohmeyer—"

"You'll be a high flyer, if you drink Strohmeyer—" my dad sang.

"Yes, that Strohmeyer."

"I thought you were friends with him," my mother said. "You went out to dinner. Worked together."

In my parents' world, dinner was something you did with friends. "It's not the same, Mama. Lawyers socialize all the time without being friends."

"So, Ted Strohmeyer," my father prompted.

"He copied a professor's article and submitted it for publication in the law review."

"You didn't publish it, did you? We taught you better—"

"Papa, no, of course not. I caught it well before it got to that stage. I turned over the documents to the dean." I fingered the green and white envelope. "I'll go to this thing and see what the school's going to do. Though I don't think it can be much."

"Not fair he should be able to claim law review if he didn't do the work. You said this is prestigious, right?"

"It's something that other lawyers think is important."

My mother made coffee and placed the pot on the table along with real cream and sugar cubes.

"I may not be some fancy lawyer," my mother prefaced, "but I think maybe you should read the letter."

I lifted the heavy stock from the table. Quickly my eyes skimmed over the contents. Sure I'd misunderstood what I'd read, I put down my roll, wiped my fingers, and held the letter with two hands and read again, this time every single word.

"I'm being summoned before the Law Review Board of Editors," I said. Disbelief filled me. What in the hell had happened? I read it a third time. "They're accusing me of dereliction of duty," I sputtered.

Dropping the letter, I turned from my mother to father and back again. Their faces were etched with concern.

"Maybe you should call your Tom?" my mother offered.

Tom thought law review was a stupid waste of time, but…. The cinnamon smell that had been welcoming was suddenly overwhelming. Appetite gone, I pushed myself from the table. Coffee sloshed on the speckled red Formica.

My mother had the towel from the oven handle on the table before I could begin to blot with the paper napkin on my lap.

"I need to go," I said.

"Okay, lieb. We'll be here."

I drove my now empty car to the law school. The front door was locked on Saturday, but my key slipped smoothly into the lock. It was reading period and the main lobby was empty save a few sleep deprived looking first-years.

I went to the law review offices, but they were empty as well. My school mailbox didn't have a thing in it. The library was filled with more students, hard at work on their laptops making outlines for final exams. But no one from the law review staff was there. I greeted a couple of the second-years I'd been working with on their comments. Their replies were polite but perfunctory.

My heart sped up. My palms grew damp with the brush-offs. I chastised myself. I was probably being irrational. No one wanted to stop and chat days before exams started. I made another circuit then decided to go back to my office. I locked myself in the small room, and dialed Tom from the heavy black telephone on my desk.

When a knock sounded on the door, I looked up at the clock. I'd been in the room for nearly an hour, and hadn't done more than sit and jiggle my leg.

"Tom," I said in relief when I let in my boyfriend. "I need your advice," I said. After showing him the letter, I waited for his outrage on my behalf, but it wasn't forthcoming.

"Wow," he said, placing the paper on Gesick's desk. "I think you need to pick the best teacher you can to defend you before the Board."

"What? Why? This must be some kind of mistake," I said. "I've been totally blindsided. I've been doing this job for the last ten or eleven months. I've stayed up nights talking second-years through panic attacks about their research and writing. I've…"

"I don't doubt your commitment, Casey. You gave this law review job more time than I ever would have."

"But they're saying I didn't do that. That I didn't do any of that."

"You're reading a lot into dereliction of duty."

"Then what do you think this is about?"

"I don't know, but I can't stay right now. I need to do some catching up. Skipped too many classes this spring, and I need to cram, okay. We'll talk in a week. Pick a professor. A good one."

8

I looked like crap while I buttoned up my light green oxford shirt. The mirror on the back of the closet in my childhood bedroom had reflected better images of me. High school prom, graduation, the moments before my parents took me out for dinner to celebrate being magna cum laude at Ohio State. All of those images of that other Casey looked better than me now.

Biting my lip with determination, I zipped up black trousers and tucked and smoothed the shirt the best I could. I considered makeup, then abandoned the thought as quickly as it had come. I wasn't looking for a date. I needed help— and not of a romantic kind—big time. Over the last two sleepless nights, I'd turned over everything in my head again and again. At best, this was some stupid mistake. At worst, I could lose my position on the law review. All the work I'd done would be for nothing. I slapped my face with my palms bringing some needed color to my cheeks. This was defeatist thinking, and it needed to stop.

I made it to the law school in record time. Instead of figuring out a bus from my parents' house, I paid the school's parking fee, which should have been outlawed instead of state sanctioned highway robbery. I added the fee to my mental list of one more thing I'd have to pay off with my first couple of Morrell Gates paychecks. Thankfully, I made it to Professor Richard Sinclair's office with fifteen minutes to spare before my nine o'clock appointment.

For ten minutes, I paced up and down the narrow hallway, trying to figure out the best way to approach the professor. At eight fifty-five, I knocked.

I was in the office before he'd finished his 'come in.'

"Casey, your message to the secretary was cryptic," Sinclair started. "You want to talk about Transnational Litigation before the final? No need to be nervous. You've always been one of my best prepared students. You lived up to your reputation."

"My reputation?"

"As one of the diligent ones. Don't think it's gone unnoticed by the faculty that you've always not only come to class regularly and on time, but you always have the day's cases briefed and prepared. You're ahead of your peers for a reason. Looks like you may graduate with honors, too."

What Sinclair said completely jibed with my own impression of myself.

"I'm the first in my family to go to college," I said, slowly moving into the cluttered office and pushing the door closed behind me. "My parents drilled into me from day one that all it takes is hard work for people to succeed in America." I reached into my backpack and pulled out the letter/summons and placed it on Sinclair's desk. "This is why I'm really quite confused about this."

My professor stared at the letter. I perched on the edge of a paper-filled seat while he rolled back in his chair then pulled something from a small drawer in his desk. Sinclair slipped reading glasses onto the end of his nose before moving the letter toward him.

"Dereliction of duty? Sounds like you were in the army and didn't scrub enough toilets to get promoted from private."

"I'm not sure what it means either," I admitted.

"I'm sorry to hear about this thing here. But the good news is that you're on track for graduation and you've got a job waiting for you. I wish I could say the same for all your fellow students. Consider yourself lucky."

"Lucky? They want to remove me from my position on law review."

"Okay."

Sinclair was entirely too laid back. He had to know how important this was. I'd dug through the faculty directory and had checked Sinclair's curriculum vitae so I knew he'd been no slouch.

"Not okay. You went to Princeton undergrad, and Columbia Law school," I said, pointing to the two framed diplomas behind him, all in Latin. "You were editor-in-chief of the law review while you were at Columbia. You have to know how important this is."

"What do you need from me?" he asked, sitting up properly in his chair.

I handed over a second sheet of paper. It was a photocopy of the law review policies.

"It says there that I can have a professor represent me. I'm asking you to do that for me. You're one of the best professors here. You have great credentials and qualifications. You were EIC of your law review. You clerked on the second circuit and for Thurgood Marshall." I hoped my words were persuasive.

My summer at Morrell Gates might have only been ten weeks, but I'd seen how a big firm intimidated a small one, not only by burying the small firm in paper. I'd seen them scare the shit out of an older solo practitioner during a deposition by loading the room with partners and associates, all top ten law school graduates. The private practitioner had folded like a cheap suit in minutes. She'd not only dismissed her case, but had agreed to pay some of the defendant's costs.

"What did you do? Cheat? Plagiarize? Sleep with one of my colleagues? I've never seen anything like this before. What could you have done to piss them off this much?"

"That's just it, though," I said on the verge of exasperation. "I didn't do anything except my job."

Professor Sinclair sighed. He looked me up and down, then glanced back at an ornate brass and wood clock on his credenza, as if he'd found me wanting somehow.

"I have half an hour."

"I'm not sure—"

"Wait," he said, removing his glasses, then holding up his flat palm toward me. "Did you rat out Ted Strohmeyer?"

"I'm not a rat. Strohmeyer's the one who did the sneaky rat-fink thing."

"This came up at the faculty meeting on Friday. A student had reported Strohmeyer for plagiarism. You're that student, aren't you?"

"What's that got to do with this?"

"Maybe something. Maybe nothing. Tell me about your tenure as ECE," he demanded, shortening my title. Law school did love the acronym.

"I'm kind of embarrassed to say it's not particularly distinguishable. I tried, but it's the same this year as last."

"The same? You tried?"

"I tried to elevate the law review. I pushed the second-years hard to write good comments, research that any law review in the country would be proud to publish."

"How was that received?"

"What?"

"Pushing the second-years?"

"Well maybe push wasn't the right word. Encourage? Supervise? Mold? I don't know. In the end, there are some really good comments. They're on diverse topics, and have a lot of original research."

"A few of which the law review will be proud to publish, no doubt."

"I hope not."

Sinclair tilted his head like a dog who was trying to figure out what humans were going on about.

"What do you mean, hope not?"

"We can't, as a school, move up in ranking unless people have heard about us, our students, our graduates. Like I did this year, I've encouraged the comment editors to submit their notes elsewhere."

Sinclair's eyebrows shot up to the ceiling.

"They agreed to that?"

"Okay, not exactly," I admitted.

"Not exactly?"

"They didn't agree at all. But I have hopes that next year's kids think outside the box."

"When's the hearing?"

"Friday. The third of May."

"I'm in the middle of preparing for exams…" Sinclair sounded like he was trying to back out, find an excuse. I wasn't going to let him do that. This was entirely too critical to me and my career.

"I wouldn't ask if it weren't important. The letter was unclear, but I think the end result of a yes vote to remove me would take me off the masthead altogether. I'd lose the ability to call myself Senior Comment Editor." When Sinclair would have spoken, I cut him off. "I know, Morrell Gates. But what if Morrell turns out like Mudge Rose?" I asked about a major New York law firm that had imploded last year. "Then I'd be out looking for a new job with a less burnished resume."

"Gotcha. Got it. I'll be there Friday." He glanced down, squinting. "At ten. In the meantime, I need you to prepare a brief outlining your tenure at the law review. What your duties were. Whether you've completed them, and so on."

Relief flooded through me. I wasn't going to have to go it alone. I now had the backing of one of the most respected professors at the school. I had a top ten, Ivy Leaguer in my corner.

"Thank you. Thank you. Thank you."

"Don't thank me yet. There's no precedence for this here. I have no idea what to expect."

"At least you've given me half a chance."

9

Tom, Lulu, and I sat on three hard plastic and metal chairs outside the small seminar room where my ten o'clock hearing was scheduled. From nine o'clock on, I watched as editor after editor walked by us and into the room innocuously numbered five-oh-three. There was little acknowledgment from editors I'd worked with for one or two years, no more than a nod in my direction from a few. Most couldn't meet my eyes.

"Geez, you've been hangin' with a bunch of haters," Lulu said when the nineteenth or twentieth person disappeared into the room.

Ten minutes before the hearing was to start, Sinclair came down the corridor, puffing, a bit out of air.

"Sorry. I know I said we should talk at nine, but I was dealing with the department secretary making copies of last years' exam instead of this one." Sinclair jerked the thumb of his empty hand toward the closed door. The other hand held a slim leather covered notebook. "What's going on in there?"

"They won't let me in until the appointed time," I said.

"Let me take stock," Sinclair said. He disappeared through the door.

"This is killing me," I said. My stomach had turned sour hours ago.

"Case," Tom started. "This doesn't make any bit of difference. You have the job. You have me. In a week or two, you won't be thinking a thing about any of this crap. Ten years from now, even less."

I turned pleading eyes the other way toward Lulu. She wasn't any more sympathetic. "He's kinda right, you know. Unless you're going to get a clerkship or teach or something, you'll be good to go irregardless."

The door opened and Sinclair waved me over.

"I've gotta go. Wish me luck?" I ended the last as a question. I didn't need luck, but a liberal application of fairness. I smoothed the lapels and skirt of my navy interview suit one last time before stepping through the door.

I started counting the moment I walked through the door. Fourteen up in the front of the room facing the student seats. Twenty more editors filled the rest. Caesar before the Roman senate had probably had it easier than this. There was no seat set aside for me or Sinclair.

Gesick offered us a place to stand before the dais.

"Do you have any opening remarks?" Gesick asked.

Opening remarks. I was supposed to have had time to study for finals and prepare something to say. I fumbled with the microphone, then my hands. I was infinitely grateful when Sinclair stepped in next to me.

"The letter you sent did not specify procedure, so I'm calling for the use of Robert's Rules of Order."

Robert's Rules were what everyone at the law school used for meetings. It was a tiny brown book on parliamentary procedure. I hated all the motioning and debating and crap that book called for. Rational adults ought to be able to have a discussion without all that. I didn't protest, though. Maybe it would keep this civil and on track.

Almost immediately, argument erupted in the room. From what I could tease out, everybody and their brother had a thought on how this could go down. Seriously? I wanted to ask them. Didn't they have something better to do than participate in a witch hunt? Like study for finals and prepare for graduation. I kept those thoughts to myself, though.

Professor Peter Haynes peeled himself from the wall he'd been holding up and stood.

"Let's not argue. We don't have all morning. Robert's Rules it is," Haynes said, and then went back to slouching. Haynes's posture was a reflection of involvement with law review. All of which added up to—not much. He'd shaken my hand at the law review dinner following the board election. He'd poked his head in our office during the holiday party. But when I'd put some of the issues of regurgitation and lack of effort on the part of second-year student comments to him, he'd nodded, then made a beeline for the buffet.

"I make a motion that Casey Cort be removed as Senior Comment Editor of the law review," Gesick said in opening.

"Second," Wyles piped in.

"On the floor for discussion," Gesick said.

In an instant, my past and future were up for debate.

"What about my opening statement?" I asked at the same time another editor, a second year started to speak.

"One at a time, Casey. He has the floor," Gesick said pointing to the second-year.

"The reason I think we need to vote Casey out is because she's been unfairly hard on us second-years. I had to rewrite my comment two different times. My first attempts, she called derivative."

"You wrote about two different circuit splits that were resolved by the Supreme Court. I tried to move you away from the tried and true."

"Casey, it's not your turn to speak," Gesick said pointing to another editor ready to air a grievance.

"I joined law review so that I could have not only a journal, but a publication on my resume," Wyles said. "I am a comment editor. But Casey's prohibition of us publishing our own notes in our own journal was the final straw."

"What prohibition? You voted me down," I said before I was drowned out by yet another editor.

"She made me rewrite my comment also," was the complaint of another second-year. "My grades went way down first semester writing one, then a second comment."

"You analyzed a case that was overturned by—"

"Casey, it's not your turn. We're following Roberts Rules, and the discussion is on the motion for removal, not why you've burdened students already at the top of the class with more work, or why your success is more important than anyone else's," Wyles said.

Wow.

Okay.

I'd had no idea that any of these people had these feelings about me. I mean sure, I knew there was some grumbling from the second-years. In the end though, their notes were twice as strong as the crop from our class.

Of course, I knew Roxy Wyles was bitter from not winning the spot of Senior Comment Editor, but watching all that curl into a ball of vitriol aimed straight at me was, frankly, awful.

Listening to the litany of complaints from my buttoned down colleagues, you'd have thought I'd spent the last eleven months torturing editors rather than missing sleep and working my butt off to make our law school one of the best we could be.

"I move to close the debate," Gesick said after nearly every editor had a chance to poke at me.

"Second," someone piped from the gallery.

"All those in favor of the motion, a show of hands."

All but three hands, one of them my own, were thrust high in the air.

"All those opposed?" I raised my hand high, only joined by one other. That other person was a second-year who'd cried in my office nearly once a week after I'd edited her comment. She wasn't crying now. But her one vote along with mine weren't enough to win the day.

"The motion is passed."

"Next order of business. I move to vote for a new Senior Comment Editor whose name will appear alone on the masthead of all issues not already in print."

"Point of Information," I said. I stood taller than before. "The previous motion was to remove me as Senior Comment Editor. Nowhere in that motion did it mention anything about invalidating the work I've done over the last eleven or so months."

"That is not a point of information request, Casey. You're making an ad hoc motion to amend," Gesick said.

"I am not. My point stands. Robert's Rules require you to clarify."

"Point of order. Point of order. The motion isn't up for debate," Wyles shouted.

"Because in a fair election, no one would choose you, Roxy. You're like a British prime minister, picked because you're the only one left standing." I hadn't meant to be mean, but it was true.

"Question of privilege," Wyles called out.

"I'm not threatening you, Roxy. No need to overreact."

"Maybe you should leave, Casey," Professor Haynes said.

"Leave. As a voting editor, I have the right to be here. Unless you're voting to remove me as an editor even though I graded on."

"Calm down, no one's kicking you off of law review. I think, however, we'd all be more comfortable if we could conduct the remaining business of the law review without your disruptive presence."

"Disruptive?" They hadn't seen disruptive.

"Yes. There's only a single motion on the floor, a new vote. We've already debated and voted on the issue of your competence," Gesick said.

"Then I move we table this discussion, and move to reconsider or rescind the first motion," I demanded. Suddenly

I was grateful for Robert's Rules. They gave me some mechanisms for fighting back, weak though they may be.

"That's a losing move, Casey, and a waste of time. Some of us still trying to beef up our GPAs need to study for finals."

"Point of order!" Sinclair shouted. I'd almost forgotten he was there. Unlike a real trial, I hadn't had a minute to defend myself, and Sinclair even less.

Gesick ignored Sinclair and turned to me instead.

"Casey?" he called, his voice soft and kind of menacing. I was really regretting not taking that self-defense class. Gesick was downright scary.

"What?" I kept my tone defiant. He couldn't do anything to me here, anything more than he'd already done.

"We don't want to have to vote to remove you. It would be best if you step out," he said, his voice soft steel. Leave or they'd strip me of law review forever. There wasn't even a reasonable choice there.

My head swiveled between Sinclair and Haynes. Both looked out of their depth. I guess I'd gotten what was coming to me. Collecting my bag, I stood and walked out of the seminar room with as much dignity as I could muster.

Lulu was sitting exactly where I'd left her.

"Where's Tom?"

"Don't know. He said he had something to do. What happened in there? Where's Sinclair?"

"I was ambushed. All the talk about procedure was for show. They wanted me out."

"At the end of the year? What, now?"

Sinclair chose that moment to emerge from the room. The double doors banged behind him.

"What now is that you're going to need to talk to the dean," Sinclair said.

"Why? They voted Roxy in, right? What is she going to do, other than publish her own comment and those of her cronies?"

"They did vote Roxy Wyles in. She's the Senior Comment Editor now. They're looking to retroactively remove you from the masthead now. That's the motion under consideration."

With that, I thought my head was going to explode. I took a deep breath and thought about the production schedule.

"There are already two issues printed. They can't take that away from me."

"Like I said, there's no precedence for this, Casey." Sinclair shrugged again. I wanted to grab him by his shoulders and shake him.

"They might not have loved the work I did while editor, but I was good. I was there. I showed up. They can't erase me like I was never an editor. What did you say?" I rounded on Sinclair.

"What was I going to say, Ms. Cort? It was a witch hunt in there. Haynes didn't do his job. Not at all. I, uh, have to get back upstairs, make sure the right exams are ready."

"I can't believe I ever had a crush on him," Lulu said to his disappearing back. "Where did he leave his backbone?"

"I think I need to get to the dean."

"What about exams? You need that diploma more than you need your name on any damn masthead. See the forest, Case. See the forest."

10

"Where have you been? I've been keeping lunch warm in the oven." That was my mother. Sometimes I wanted to tell her that food wasn't love. Instead, I hefted a large Office Max bag onto the kitchen table. "Had to get this to help me study for finals," I lied.

My dad slid the bulky box from the bag. The laptop computer's doppelganger, a shiny professional photo highlighting its utilitarian beauty stared up at us from the box.

"A computer? I thought you used the school's computers," my dad said.

"I used the ones at law review, Dad. I can't exactly show my face in there right now."

"Why not?"

"The people who are taking over are using them." It was the best excuse I could come up with. I hadn't yet told them about the masthead issue. The dean was in Iowa and unavailable for meetings, but I was hoping to get to him by e-mail. Some students had found that sending a message from your computer to theirs yielded a better response than telephones and old-fashioned visits, which if timed incorrectly, never seemed to reach the intended target.

"Looks complicated," my dad said, fingering the slotted tab on the side of the box. I plucked it open and removed the computer from its Styrofoam confines. It was heavier than I'd imagined. The little 'Q' logo was cute. If pressed, I'd probably have to admit it had been the deciding factor to buy a Compaq. I'd liked the little cow one, but the delay between ordering and delivery was too long for my immediate needs—keep what I had earned.

"It'll be good, I think."

Before I could grab it, my dad latched on to the receipt that had floated from the bag.

"Four thousand dollars? Casey Ann Cort. That's practically a down payment on a house."

"It's an investment in my future, Dad. I'll be able to use it for working in the fall. If I bill a lot of hours, I will probably get a bonus that covers the cost."

"My God, an education on credit is one thing. They can't ever take that away from you. But a computer? You've managed to do pretty well without this."

Before the lecture went on, I took my bowl of potato salad with sausage and my new computer upstairs. Once I closed the door to my room, I cleaned off my desk and unplugged my telephone. After I got the computer booted and running, I inserted one of the disks the store clerk had given me. A thousand hours and one month of free Internet, it promised. Again, I entered my credit card number.

Hopefully, it would never get to the point where I had to renew and my charge was rejected faster than the speed of sound. I would never share with my parents that I took out store credit for the computer. I'd directed the bills to Summit Avenue, so they'd never see those. It would all be worth it, I promised myself. Come September, I'd pay everything off.

It took thirty minutes, but I was finally logged into CSU's system. I looked at the dean's e-mail I'd scribbled on a piece of paper during the second unfruitful visit to his office when Della told me he'd be in Iowa up until commencement.

Scribbling out a bunch of different messages, I finally settled on one and typed.

```
FROM:      Casey Cort
TO:        Dean Condit
DATE:      May 4, 1996
SUBJECT:   Law Review Masthead
```

Dean Condit,
As you may be aware, I have been removed from my position as Senior Comment Editor by a simple majority vote of the board. The decision was without basis or merit. Professor Sinclair suggested I contact you regarding my right to appeal my ouster.
For your review, I've attached a copy of the brief I prepared on my behalf before last week's hearing.
I look forward to your response.
Casey Cort

While I was typing that e-mail, the computer chirped, alerting me to another e-mail coming my way. I sent the one to Dean Condit, then opened the newest.

```
FROM:      Prof. Sinclair
TO:        Casey Cort
SUBJECT:   Mediation
DATE:      May 4, 1996
```

Ms. Cort,
I've spoken with Erwin Gesick this morning. He's proposing that you remain a Comment Editor rather than a General Editor. He says this reflects the work you've done and will allow you to continue to work with students you are now helping. For those issues not printed, you will not be Senior Comments Editor on the masthead. I have a faculty meeting in an hour. Please let me know if you can accept this proposal in the next hour. Erwin Gesick needs an answer before 5:00 PM today.

I pushed the top of the new laptop shut. The smell of new plastic rolled off the computer in waves. A few months ago, this would have been a fun purchase. I would have poked around on the Internet that everyone was so fascinated with. Maybe I would have jumped into a chat group or discussion about something interesting. But this recent purchase was bringing me nothing but bad news. With every day that passed, I was losing ground. A couple of months ago, I'd been on top of the world, and now I was clawing my way back to what was rightfully mine.

The chime sounded again. I resisted the urge to toss the four grand machine against the wall.

```
FROM:      Dean Condit
To:        Casey Cort
Subject:   Mediation
Date:      May 4, 1996


It is my understanding that you have been
offered the opportunity to settle your dis-
pute with the law review. Please respond to
Erwin Gesick's proposal before end of busi-
ness today. I will enforce the agreement
reached.
```

"My dispute? My dispute!" I yelled to the empty room. I didn't have a damned dispute. One day I was doing my work and the next day I was being pushed off the law review. There wasn't a single discernible reason this was happening. Not a single one. How some second-years could get their panties in a bunch over well-deserved criticism, I couldn't fathom.

I pinched the phone cord and removed it from the computer and inserted it back into my cordless phone. I pressed the button. Dial tone. Good. My parents didn't use the phone much, but my mother could sometimes settle in for an extensive chat with one of her friends from the parish.

The numbers under my fingers were as familiar as my own. Lulu answered on the first ring.

"Do you think I should sue?"

"Sue? Casey? Sue who?"

"The law school. Remember Administrative Law. What they're trying to do makes no sense. They've followed no procedures, and now the dean is leaving my fate up to Erwin Gesick."

"The way you say that, it sounds like it's bad."

"I don't know if he ever liked me, but this is a shit way of showing it," I said, then caught her up on the latest round of e-mails.

"So back to suing. What are you talking about?"

"I have to do something. They're trying to railroad me."

"Casey, I'm not like you. Graduation is not assured unless I buckle down and memorize these damned cases. I'd really like to help you, but I can barely think about anything but this first exam for Tax Exempt Organizations. I love you, hon. I trust you to do what's best."

After we hung up, I turned off the laptop and packed it in my bag. I needed to talk to someone outside of the crazy law school world. I knew just the person.

11

"This is a surprise," Miriam Shively greeted me near the entrance to her office door. Her secretary nodded in greeting then went back to typing whatever she was hearing from dictation headphones glued to her ears.

"Thanks for seeing me on such short notice." I shook Shively's hand.

"You're about four months early. We don't have your office ready...just yet."

I forced myself to laugh along with the lawyer's attempt at humor, even though I was in anything but a laughing mood.

"Come on back to my office. We can talk there."

Shively's secretary paused typing long enough to offer me coffee. I asked for water instead. I didn't need caffeine making me any more jumpy than I already was.

I sat in one chair, laid my bag, bulky with the new computer in the other. After Shively's secretary brought tea for her and water for me, I let go of the breath I'd been holding.

"Are exams all done?" she asked. "I remember the itch for it to be finally over in that last semester of law school."

"They start today, actually."

"My God, what are you doing here? Did you take all seminars or something?"

"I have two exams later this week. I kind of wanted to ask your advice on a problem I'm having."

"What kind of advice?" she asked. I'd been intentionally vague on the phone.

"Legal? I guess."

"Am I going to need to run a conflicts check?"

"Not exactly..."

"You've got me worried that you're about to face the death penalty. Wait a sec." Shively told her secretary that she was in official DND mode and to hold non-essential calls.

"I'm not going to jail."

"If you were, that handsome boyfriend of yours would surely get you out. Is he still going over to the prosecutor's office?"

I answered even though I was itching to get on with my problems. "He's starting about the same time as me."

"Have your bar trip planned?"

I nodded then looked away. Tears were starting and no way did I want this almost partner at Morrell Gates to see that. Having one of my future bosses see me cry was not a great start to a career where I needed to be taken seriously.

"Casey. Look at me. Do you remember what I told you about client management this summer?"

I turned back to Shively, but shook my head. "I...sorry...I don't remember."

"The reason we offer clients coffee and water and pastry is not because we're looking to compete with the cafe downstairs. It's because we want clients to be comfortable discussing their problems. I can see, though, I'm making you anything but comfortable. Let's talk." She opened her hands in an expansive gesture.

"They're trying to kick me off law review," I confessed.

"Well that's not jail. But it is serious. Tell me more."

So I told her, the short sordid tale of how discouraging publication of our own notes and riding the second-years hard, for their own good, had somehow alienated every last one of my fellow editors.

"What's the school's appeal process?"

"Somewhere between murky and none." I hoisted my laptop from my bag and opened it on Shively's desk. "I hope you don't mind," I said as I lifted the lid and brought up the e-mails. Shively came around the desk and looked over my shoulder.

"So they are trying to get you to agree to take yourself off the review and the masthead because that's what this Erwin Gesick, your EIC wants. But if you want to appeal, they're not sure they have jurisdiction. I got that right?"

"Exactly."

"What did you do to piss off your EIC?"

"Refuse to hook up with him."

"Hook up?"

"Date, see, have dinner, have sex. Some or all of the above. At least that's my friend's analysis. I've had a boyfriend the whole time I was on law review."

Shively walked back to her side of the desk and sunk into her chair. "Wow. Venues change. Clothes change. Men don't. I hate to say it, but this is just a taste of what it's like, Casey. This is why I pulled you aside last summer to slip into a Women's Initiative meeting. We have to band together to put a stop to this kind of thing. Anyway, let's see what we can do."

Two hours later, Shively had helped me write a complaint and a slew of other documents I could file with the Common Pleas court. Documents that would hopefully put a stop to the process Gesick had set into motion.

"That was harder than I thought," I said, no longer embarrassed about my lack of knowledge of the practical side of the law. Last summer had lifted the veil from my eyes so to speak.

Law school was not lawyer school. It was why I was here now.

"Casey, before you run down to the clerk's office half cocked, please think hard about what you're going to do."

I sat back, confused. "But you said when we started that women can't take what's doled out to them. That we need to be strong, stay together, fight back."

"I did say those things. But have you looked at me? Where am I sitting right now?"

"In a thirty-fifth floor office overlooking Tower City. Working on your own cases."

"I'm not a partner," Shively said as if she was revealing she was homeless.

"It's hard to make partner, isn't it?" To me partners were the old gray-haired men who didn't so much talk as nod and walk to their oversized offices and make whatever magic paid for seven floors in one of Cleveland's highest buildings.

"Let's see. I've been here eleven years. I oversee toxic tort litigation that no partner wants to do. They'll happily take the billing and responsible attorney credit, but my biggest client has capped fees. It's two million dollars a year if I bill two thousand hours. It's two million dollars a year if I bill three thousand hours."

Two million dollars in billings sounded like a whole lot to me.

"Are you up for partner?" I asked tentatively.

"I was. Last year. I didn't make it. I'm 'Of Counsel' now."

"What does that mean?" I hadn't paid much attention to any of these politics over the summer. My single-minded goal had been to get through the summer and get an offer.

"I have an employment contract. I don't get profits. And I don't dare have any kids."

I very much wanted kids and maybe to be partner someday. For a long moment, trepidation about my future made me shiver.

"Will filing this take me off the partnership track? Won't law review removal take me off too?"

"What I'm saying, Casey, is that every action has consequences. Most times there's no predicting what all the consequences might be."

I was about to ask Shively what the consequences were that had made her Of Counsel instead of partner, but a knock on her door scuttled my opportunity.

"Miri, Dad's here," a voice said as the sound of hinges squeaked.

I turned around to greet the visitor.

Ted Strohmeyer. His head, full of thick dark hair, poked around the door.

"Casey, you're the last person I expected to see," Strohmeyer said.

His greeting was friendly. Friendlier than I'd expected. I was guessing the dean hadn't reached out to him.

"Good to see you, Ted." I stood and did the awkward handshake hug thing that seemed appropriate for people of our acquaintance, not quite co-workers, not quite friends.

"Miri." Strohmeyer tapped his gold watch. "Eleven-thirty. We need your expertise in dealing with the city on this one. The folks in Brighthill are claiming the brewery is contaminating the water supply."

"I'll be there in a moment, Ted."

"Casey," he said, tipping his head before he scuttled out of the doorway.

"Finally getting some business from the Strohmeyers? That's great," I enthused.

"For the billing partners, sure. I'll have the unenviable job of babysitting Ted, and his dad." The way she said that suggested the apple hadn't fallen far from the tree.

"Look, I know you've got to go. I can't thank you enough for helping me out. I'll think carefully about what you said. I have some studying to do today anyway, so I'll sleep on it." I packed away the papers she'd printed, that needed only my signature, as well as a liberal application of courage. "I'd keep an eye on Ted if I were you," I said, ready to reciprocate.

"Why?"

"He gets away with murder." I laughed awkwardly. "Not murder. He plagiarized his entire comment, then submitted it for publication. Pretty brazen."

Miriam Shively sat back in her seat. She gestured for me to do so as well.

"Who have you told about this?"

"Tom, my best friend Lulu. She's at the law school."

"That's it?"

"I turned the comment and its doppelganger over to the dean. But I don't think Dean Condit did anything. Ted didn't seem like anything was wrong when he stuck his head in."

"If I were you, I'd keep that stuff about Ted Strohmeyer under my hat."

"I wasn't his editor or anything. I've got clean hands here." I lifted my empty palms in demonstration.

Miriam stood, ending our meeting.

"I'm going to be late. Let me know what you decide."

12

Professor Sinclair's exam was a piece of cake. Even with minimal studying, I was sure I'd pass with flying colors. The only other exam on my schedule, Environmental Law and Regulation, was now a take-home exam. The papers due on my other seminars I'd completed and turned in early. In spite of the charges lodged against me, I did, in fact, practice what I preached. I wrote and rewrote, making sure everything I did was the best it could possibly be.

I looked at the four essay questions on the take-home. The last school exam I would ever take. There should have been some kind of elation over this last hurdle and milestone. But I couldn't wrap my head around CERCLA or the hypothetical Hispanic community that was about to be downwind of an artificial rubber plant that was, in true law school exam style, about to spew volatile organic compounds, contaminated water, and other toxic crap right onto an elementary school playground. Not to mention the rare and endangered species that would be wiped out in the name of corporate growth and progress.

I resisted handwriting, 'bad, bad corporation' on the exam and turning that in because I needed a passing grade. The professor was looking for a thoughtful, well-reasoned answer as to the claims of the poor citizens of the fictional town and the best defenses of the faceless corporate giant, the kind I'd be representing in four months' time.

Shoving the exam aside, I lifted the lid of the new laptop and booted it up. Five minutes later, I connected to the school. A list of unread emails demanded my attention.

Starting in reverse chronological order, I clicked the first.

```
FROM:      Dean Condit
TO:        Casey Cort
RE:        Your Appeal
DATE:      May 6, 1996
```
I have circulated a short note and your brief and memoranda to the faculty. If any one of them wish to take up the issue, they are free to do so at the next faculty meeting.

Wow, that was a lot of words to say nothing really. I clicked on the next e-mail.

```
FROM:      Dean Condit
TO:        Casey Cort
RE:        Faculty Review
```

DATE: May 6, 1996
It appears that one professor, Carolann
Bynum, wants to review the matter at the next
faculty meeting, to be held tomorrow May 7,
1996. I will submit the matter to them.

More, nothing.

FROM: Dean Condit
TO: Casey Cort
RE: No Jurisdiction
DATE: May 7, 1996
After consultation by and with the faculty,
I have determined that I have no jurisdiction
to oversee this matter. Any decision of the
Law Review Editorial Board is final.

I tapped my finger on the blue nub that substituted for a
mouse. Then, I moved my finger along the track pad, but
there wasn't anything further from the dean. With that single paragraph, he'd swatted me and all the work I'd done
away like a pesky fly.

Moving the cursor down, I scrolled to the next emails,
though I knew, even without clicking, that it would be like
beating a dead horse.

FROM: Professor Sinclair
TO: Casey Cort
RE: Your Appeal
DATE: May 7, 1996
Dean Condit has said he's informed you of
the faculty's decision. I'm sorry this has

happened to you. My office door is open if you want to talk.

```
FROM:      Eriwn Gesick
TO:        Casey Cort
RE:        Succession
DATE:      May 7, 1996
```

Thank you for your service to the law review. Please clean out your desk by end of business today. Roxy needs the space to engineer the transition from her to the next editor to be elected next week. Several second-years would like to continue working with you and need your assistance on the final polish before elevation votes next week. I've given them your e-mail address and home phone number. Roxy Wiles will appear on Issues 3 through 6 for Volume 45.

Have a good summer.

P.S. Please leave the office key in the pencil drawer of my desk.

Dean Condit had virtually closed the door on my future, locked it, and thrown away the key. Gathering up my bag and a cardigan that didn't look too baggy, I marched down to the kitchen.

My parents were there in companionable silence. I wasn't going to be able to slip past them out the door. I'd lost all anonymity and privacy the minute I'd moved back into my old room.

"Lieb, where are you going so soon? You've just walked in the door. I'm making Stroganoff."

"I'll be back before dinner," I promised. Because the clerk's office closed promptly at 4:30. "In plenty of time, I promise."

13

I sat in my parked car under the courthouse until my heart stopped beating so fast that I couldn't breathe. Until my hands stopped shaking enough for me to shift the pages from my messenger bag to my desk and check them one last time.

In the weak garage light, I stared at the documents. Shively had instructed me to take the Complaint for Declaratory Judgment and Temporary Restraining Order to the clerk's office. If all went according to plan, three or four hours from now, I'd walk out of the courthouse Senior Comment Editor for all six issues of the law review, the judge having declared that everything that had happened in the last weeks was illegal. Then the rest of my life could move on like I'd planned, having survived this little bump in the road.

Resolved, I stacked everything neatly in my bag then made my way to the Justice Center. As I entered the clerk's office, I immediately regretted not taking one of those clinic courses. The kind that had you representing real people with real problems. Once I'd secured a summer job at Morrell Gates, I knew that individual representation would never be on my radar. Morrell and all the other big firms in town had people who did this part, the filing, the docketing, all of the menial details.

The irony had not escaped me. I lingered at the back of the room for a good ten minutes, shifting my eyes between a possible escape via the front door and the pay phones in the corner. I desperately wanted to call Tom or Lulu or anyone for support. But it wouldn't be right to disturb my friends during their final exam period. Plus I was heeding Shively's advice.

An emergency temporary restraining order was one of the few kinds of relief granted with a judge hearing only one side. It was an anomaly in the adversarial system. If I shared this with any of my friends, Shively said, the chances of Dean Condit and Erwin Gesick getting a leg up on me increased exponentially.

I looked at the large clock ticking on the wall. Every minute I wasted was a minute I wasn't past this crater-sized bump in the road. Squaring my shoulders, I walked over to what looked like an intake desk and stood in line.

"You need to get a number back there." A harried man in a suit pointed his thumb toward a ticket machine that wouldn't have been out of place on a deli counter.

Stepping back out of line, I pulled a ticket. It was ten minutes before my number was called. I approached the county employee with my stack in hand. She pulled it from me and started pulling out rubber stamps. Ka-chung went the first stamp, adding the date to each front page. Another stamp came out, adding a case number. I watched in fascination. There was no look of recrimination or wonder at any of the documents. Like the dean and plagiarism, this was probably a daily fodder for this woman.

"How are you paying the filing fee?"

"How much?"

The clerk looked down at a laminated sheet affixed to her desk. "Two hundred fifty plus…" She appeared to be counting the number of defendants on the complaint. "Plus eighty. Three thirty total."

I wrote a check and gave her half of what my tenant had paid over to me. So much for saving money living back at home.

"Here's your judge," she said. A sharp letter opener sliced through a cube and a Post-it size piece of paper was lifted from the thick deck. She spun a caddy full of stamps, picked one, then started the stamping process all over again. Since she wasn't looking at me, I took the square paper and looked at the name.

Patrick Brody.

Oh, God.

Oh, God.

Oh, God.

The panic that had subsided came back full force. I got lightheaded for a long minute then came back to myself.

"I know this judge," I said.

The clerk didn't stop the clicking of her latest stamp. "Don't we all."

"No. Um, how do I get a new judge?"

She paused. "You related by blood or marriage?"

"No."

"Then you don't. Got an issue, take it up with the judge."

When she was done with all the work on her end, she met my eyes. "You going to walk this through?"

Remembering Shively's explicit instructions to get this in front of a judge before I left the building, I nodded. "Yes."

"Here are the copies of your motion. Take them up to judge's chambers, tell them you have an Emergency TRO, then wait. Anything else?"

Shively had told me that service was handled by the clerk's office, all cleanly by certified mail. It was a system that sounded far easier than other states with the hiring of process servers or having to jump out of the bushes to hand defendants papers. I couldn't think of a single solitary thing I'd need from the clerk's office right now.

"No," I said emphatically. "I'll just take these then." I took my TRO and left the desk. Before I could organize my bag, I looked back to see the clerk was already on to the next person.

Justice was a business like any other.

14

The ascending elevator was surprisingly slow. It stood in sharp contrast to the efficiency I'd witnessed down below. All the way up, I mulled over Shively's advice. If telling Tom was letting the cat out of the bag, pleading my case to his father would be like letting a whole pride of lions out of the cage.

When the lift clanged to a stop and the door whooshed open, I had no choice but to get off. After I perused the directory, I followed the signs to presiding judge, Patrick Brody's courtroom.

The wood paneled room was empty. No one was in the jury box, behind the bar or in front of it. Of course, the judge and his staff were probably in his chambers...somewhere. When I thought about it for more than a moment, it was only logical that the courtroom wasn't filled a la an episode of Law and Order or L.A. Law. Thinking back to those shows, though, gave me a clue. The ersatz lawyers in their slick suits and shiny hair were often filmed huddled in a judge's chambers trying to nudge justice in their client's direction. It was only a matter of figuring out where that was.

I spun on my conservative low heel, ready to make an exit and look for another door when a throat cleared. I looked back around.

"Hello," I said.

"Can I help you?"

"I'm looking for Judge Brody's chambers. I have to give him something."

The woman, heavy files in hands, stepped back. "Judges can't accept any gifts."

"No, no. Sorry. I'm here pro se. Well, I'm a law student. Um."

"Why don't you follow me," she said, turning and disappearing through a door to the left of the judge's chair. After a beat, I was right on her heels.

The back looked like a regular office building, carpeted corridor, glass-fronted offices. She led me into a large office with three desks. Though the justice center was the usual unattractive seventies vintage building, the offices were nice. My heels were silent on the plush blue carpet.

The courtroom assistant deposited the files on the floor then took up residence behind one of the desks. She gestured to the papers in my hand.

"What do you have for the judge?"

Warily, I held my stack of documents so they hovered over the desk. This was, I guess, the moment of truth. No turning back.

"It's an emergency temporary restraining order."

She gave the 'gimme' move with her hand and I handed over the papers.

The assistant put on a couple of those rubber fingers and skated through the pile.

"The judge will need the complaint and the supporting documents."

I handed over another thick stack of paper. While she paged though those, I eyed the church-quiet room. This wasn't what came to mind when someone uttered the word justice.

"Ms. Cort. Please have a seat right out there. I'll give these to the judge. He'll look them over and call you in for argument. Do you have a judgment entry prepared?"

I fumbled again for more paper, grateful that Shively had prepared me for this. I gave over the document, which stopped the law review from removing me from my duties and from the masthead. If the judge signed it as-is I had a pure win. Shively had said that the less work a judge had to do the better. If you came prepared, more often than not, it was easier for them to rule your way. As I took a seat, I hoped it was true.

Before I could get comfortable or shake out my nerves, the judge's assistant called me in.

"Judge Brody will see you now."

A door I hadn't noticed before was open. I could see Tom's dad, sitting behind a huge desk. He was looking at something on his desk and frowning. God help me if it was my motion he was pissed off about.

"Your Honor," I said tentatively as I walked into the room.

"Casey. Close that door." I turned around and did as I was told. "I have to say these aren't the circumstances under which I expected to see you."

"Nor I you." Somehow I didn't think engagement party images were flashing through his mind.

"Please have a seat."

The judge had a magnificent view of Cleveland, the now empty Browns stadium and the lake. Once I took one of the two seats in front of his desk, I had a view of the Ohio Revised Code and the man I hoped would be my father-in-law one day soon.

"Casey, I'm going to tell you that I see a lot here, day in and day out. Defendants who come to court intoxicated, companies that hide documents, plaintiff's attorneys who file nuisance suits. I even have the occasional pro se litigant. But in my years on the bench, you've managed to stump me.

"When Tom asked me to call in the favor to the Junior Arthur Gates, I was happy to do it. You're a smart girl who's got a great job and future, but these papers make it look like you're tossing all that in a bin. Judge and litigant aside, tell me what's going on. We're practically family, and this is the first I'm hearing about this?"

The weight of the world dropped from my shoulders in an instant. Tom's dad did in a few sentences what no one, not Lulu or Tom, not my parents, hadn't been able to do. Assure me that this was all going to be okay.

For the first time since it had began, I teared up. Before the trickle could turn into a waterfall, I grabbed a couple of tissues from Judge Brody's desk and did my best to stop the tingly nose and watery eyes.

"Tom and Lulu—that's my best friend—think I should walk away."

"If you're sitting here, you obviously disagree. I don't want to know what Tom or this Lulu thinks. I want to know the events that led up to this. You coming in here asking me to slap an injunction on the Cleveland Law Review and…" his fingers ticked down the page, "…more than a dozen other defendants."

I looked toward the windows again. A black robe and suit jacket, carefully draped on strong wooden hangers, hung from a wooden coat rack. Part of me wished he had on the robe. It would make the confessional nature of what I was about to say easier. I took a deep breath and started from the beginning.

"I did three things to piss off Erwin Gesick."

"Who is he?"

"Editor-in-chief of the law review."

"What's the first?"

"I turned him down for a date."

"I don't—"

"More like fifty dates. He's been slandering Tom, trying to get us to break up. His latest is that he's saying Tom likes strippers…well, hookers."

Judge Brody leaned back in his chair. His blue eyes pierced mine.

"Go on."

"I've been riding the second-years a little hard, maybe. I want them to do their best work. Law school isn't a time to slouch. Crappy research and sloppy work do not represent the school well."

"The other students complained to this Gesick?"

"Apparently so. They think my criticisms were harsh."

"You said there was a third?"

"Erwin thinks I went over his head in reporting plagiarism to the dean."

"Did you?"

"What?"

"Go over his head?"

"The law school honor code requires all misconduct be reported. One of the first things on the list is plagiarism, right after cheating on an exam."

"Who plagiarized what?"

For the first time since I'd come to his office, I hesitated. Right then I regretted bringing Ted Strohmeyer into this. I hadn't mentioned him in my moving papers. I still wasn't sure that whole thing was related to this at all, but it was starting to look like it had to be. Otherwise, none of this made sense. No Roxy Wyles power grab should have mushroomed to these proportions.

"Ted Strohmeyer, your honor. He wrote a comment...no, he stole a comment from a professor in Indiana and passed it off as his own. I was even thinking of publishing it until I checked it out. I know Tom said your families' relationship was important. I told Tom about it before I reported it to the dean."

"Is that so?"

"He said at the Advocate's Ball that the Strohmeyer relationship was important to you, so I went ahead and put his submission to the top of the pile. But I'm getting sidetracked. The Strohmeyer thing doesn't have anything to do with this."

"I see." The chair springs creaked as Brody leaned forward again. He pressed a button on the phone. "Get Shari in here, please."

A knock sounded and a court reporter carrying a transcription machine came in. She sat in a folding chair by the judge's desk and quickly set up.

"We're on the record in Casey Cort vs. Warren Condit, et al. This is an ex-parte motion for a temporary restraining order. Appearing before me, pro se, is Casey Cort. Ms. Cort, please argue your motion."

My mouth went dry. I thought I'd have more time. I thought Judge Brody would have told me we were going on the record. Suddenly, I wasn't comfortable any longer.

"I...uh..."

"Ms. Cort."

"Sorry. I..." Shari's typing when I talked, stopping when I stopped, was disconcerting.

"Your motion, Ms. Cort. While the court understands that you are a pro se plaintiff, you're an honors law student graduating in a few weeks. You should be prepared to argue a motion, especially one that you filed."

"Of course. Right. On May third of this month, the Cleveland Law Review held a hearing to remove me from my post as Senior Comment Editor. They cited as their basis, my quote, dereliction of duty, my failure to perform, in good faith, the duties of my office. As I stated to you earlier, I have more than adequately discharged my duties as Senior Comment Editor for volume forty-five. I have advised the second-years on their writing assignments. I have overseen the selection of comments for publication. I have, out of fairness, even removed my own comment from consideration.

"Why I am here today, Your Honor, is because Gesick has proposed to the dean that I be removed from the masthead for the remaining issues ready to go to the printer despite the fact that my removal hearing occurred a mere month before graduation. There is literally nothing else to be done on the review except hold an election for elevation of the second-years and transition the work over. Bottom line, your honor, I did the work, and I should receive the credit."

"That's all well and good, Ms. Cort, but why do you think you're entitled to extraordinary relief?"

"If you review the attached exhibits, you'll see that Dean Condit has refused appellate jurisdiction. This leaves me without an adequate remedy in equity or at law."

"What harm will you suffer if I don't grant your temporary restraining order?"

"I will lose the prestige and honor of having served as an officer on law review."

"Is there any proposal to remove you from law review altogether?"

"No."

"If you're removed as Senior Comment Editor, what happens?"

"I'll either be demoted to Comment Editor or General Editor."

"What impact will that have?"

"It could make it less likely that I could find a job in the future."

"Do you have a job now?"

"I am scheduled to start at Morrell Gates in September."

"What other impact will it have?"

"It could, possibly, reflect poorly on my character application to the bar."

"Is there any other way this could affect you?"

"The possible effects are too ephemeral and maybe innumerable to mention, but that doesn't take away the underlying unfairness of the school's decision not to interfere with what may be people acting on personal vendettas."

"I sympathize with you, Ms. Cort, but I'm going to go ahead and decline to issue a temporary restraining order. There hasn't been a sufficient showing today to issue a prior restraint on the respondents' right to call and conduct a meeting pursuant to the law review's and law school's code. This denial does not stand as a dismissal of your case. After the hearing occurs and if negative action is taken, you can then schedule a full motion hearing before the court where arguments from both sides will be heard and a determination would be made if you've suffered any deprivation of rights." To Shari, the court reporter he said, "That's it. The rest is off the record."

I pressed the tissues to my face again, trying to relieve the pressure that was increasing around my eyes and nose. I'd lost spectacularly. What I had thought was a sympathetic ear had turned deaf to my problems. I wanted to shout that I wasn't a Brody, not yet anyway. My reputation was all I had. But I suspected that if I wanted to be a Brody, my thoughts were best kept to myself.

"Casey. This is no way to start your law career. Sometimes you have to take your knocks. I'm more than happy to grant a dismissal of your action should you choose. I'm sure the clerk's office could halt service. You could go home, graduate, and put this all behind you." Judge Brody looked at his watch. "It's ten to four. Let me know before four fifteen what you want to do."

15

Of course, I'd dismissed the suit. When the presiding judge and your father-in-law to be told you to kill your lawsuit against your dean and the law review editors who were out to get you, you did. I was beginning to think Tom had been right all along.

Law review wasn't life or death. It wasn't even the difference between being unemployed or not. I'd keep Senior Comment Editor on my resume. I defied anyone to challenge that I hadn't done the work to deserve the title.

With my dream job in my sights, though, I may never have to do the job search thing again. Graduation was tomorrow, and law school would be behind me.

"I think you should wear the white one, lieb," my mother said, jarring me from my thoughts. She wrung her hands. I could see her and myself in the mirror. The moment was a reflection of many in my life, only this time I was an adult, soon to have a doctorate degree. My mother's immigrant fear of saying or wearing the wrong thing hadn't changed though.

I didn't turn away from the full-length mirror in my childhood bedroom. Mom and I had been to Filene's Basement on Friday. I was wearing one of the two dresses we'd purchased. I stared and tried to figure out what would be best.

"But I'm going to the Morrell Gates reception after commencement. Don't you think the red would make more of a statement?"

"From what you tell me these stuffy law firm types aren't looking for a statement. Why don't you save that for your swearing in ceremony?"

"Don't jinx it, Mom. A lot of people don't pass the bar on their first try." I felt like an Olympian with one successful heat behind her and another deciding heat up ahead.

"I'm not worried. You succeed at everything you do. A lawyer in the family," she crowed. "I can't believe it. Can you come to mass with me tonight at St. Ignatius? We could go to the late service."

She wanted to show me off, her daughter the soon to be law school graduate. Normally, I'd even indulge her and shake Father Boyle's hand, gossip with the little old Irish ladies who not-so-discreetly socialized in the last pew during service.

"I have to pack, Mom. The guy who is subletting from me agreed to give me run of the place tonight while he was out. I can get my winter clothes and figure out what furniture I'm going to take with me."

The mirror reflected a frown creasing the space between my mother's brows.

"We're very modern, Casey, but still your dad and I are uncomfortable with this living in sin. Why hasn't Tom asked you to marry him?"

"Do you want me to ask him, Mom?" I cut my eyes at her. Propriety would stop her dead in her tracks. I don't think she'd yet recovered from me asking a boy to prom instead of waiting for an invitation.

"No. No, of course not. You can't ask a boy that. Your dad and I would feel better about this if you had a ring. Then we'd know he was serious."

"I think asking me to move in together is serious. I think booking a first class bar trip is serious, Mom. It's not perfect. I'd like to be engaged too. Who knows, maybe I will be today or even next week. I think he's waiting for the perfect time to pop the question."

"When will that be?"

"You always said I should be patient. I'm trying to do that. In the meantime, can you help me pick a dress?"

"Wear the white one. Maybe it'll jog his memory that he's supposed to propose."

It didn't do much for my eyes, the simple fitted dress peppered with tiny cabbage roses. But it did camouflage my hips and the bias cut across the chest made me look like I had one. I nodded toward my mother's reflection.

"You're right, this one." It was throwing her a bone, but anything to deflect her from marriage and babies, I'd take. Maybe I'd save the red for the night Tom would finally kneel and say he had something very important to ask.

My mother sat heavily on my bed as I carefully stepped from the dress and put it back on the sturdy plastic hanger it had come on.

The cuckoo clock my dad had given me on my twelfth birthday announced it was two o'clock.

"You wound it?" my mother looked at the black forest girl moving back and forth in her makeshift swing.

"I do love it."

"Maybe you should take it with you to Tom's house," she said. I heard the concession in her voice. It was a big deal that my mom had come on board. I hugged her. She was warm as always and smelled slightly of apples. I'd miss them so much when I moved out.

"I'm glad we had this time together," I said, fishing my jeans from the floor. I pulled them on, then added a tur-quoise pocket T-shirt.

"You going to the house on Summit now?"

"I'm supposed to meet Tom there at two-thirty."

"Go. Go. Maybe he wants to talk about more than furni-ture arranging."

I leaned in and kissed her again, on the forehead this time. My heart filled to bursting with love for these people who'd gotten me to where I was, and with love for the man with whom I was going to spend my life. Law review was just a stupid bump in the road. Family and friends were what mattered.

I ran down the stairs and grabbed my keys from the little wooden table by the door. The drive from West Boulevard to Summit Avenue was quick. Maybe Tom and I would in-vite my parents over after I moved in but before bar classes started. They'd love the place. My dad always had a fond-ness for Lake Erie.

Tom's car was already in the driveway. This time I pulled up next to his car instead of parking in the street. Would I take the right side of the garage and him the left?

My boyfriend opened the door before I even knocked.

"Hey, are there two different garage door openers?"

"Hey, Case," Tom said and backed away from the door when I leaned in to kiss him.

"Sorry. Hi, how are you would probably have been better. I got excited about parking in the garage and staying out of the snow. I've been scraping and brushing so many mornings and I won't miss it. Do you think we should get a snowplow contract before all the good guys get booked up? Do you have a lawn guy?"

I stopped talking when I noticed that Tom hadn't responded to a single question. The enthusiasm in the house was entirely one-sided.

"We need to talk, Case. I thought we could go out on the deck."

My heart sped up, and I balled my fists in anticipation. I stepped out on the deck. The rainbow Adirondack chairs and complementary wood tables were growing on me. They'd seemed old fashioned and stuffy the first time I'd come to the house. But now I could see myself sitting in the green, yellow, blue, or red chairs. Maybe I'd keep a lemonade on the pastel side tables.

Tom was behind me. He closed the door, probably to keep it cool inside. It was at least eighty degrees today, though the breeze off the lake dried the sweat on my face.

"I'm going over to North Moreland tonight. I promised the guy subletting that I'd clear out my stuff. He's interested in taking over the lease. Did I mention he's a medical student? Wants to be near, but not too near, Cleveland Clinic."

"I don't know how best to say this, Casey," Tom said. His voice was grave.

"Is your...are your mom and dad okay?" I whispered the question. I tried to remember if I'd glanced at the Plain Dealer this morning. Surely if something had happened to one of the Brodys it would have been on the front page. My mother would have told me. It couldn't have been that bad.

"My parents are fine, actually. They're looking forward to graduation tomorrow."

"So are my mom and dad. Dad's all worried about what he's going to wear. He says his suit is too funereal, but he got rid of a bunch of clothes when he stopped working."

"We can't move in here together."

"Oh. Oh." I turned toward the water, away from Tom. God, I hope disappointment didn't show on my face. I'd woven so many fantasies about our life together, starting in this place. I imagined we'd tell our kids about the Summit Avenue house where we'd been young and in love, but had moved to something more practical when they'd come along.

"Does your uncle need to move back in? Your mom want to rent it? I haven't signed over the lease yet. We could move into my place in Shaker Square. It's not like this, but it's got two bedrooms. You'll get used to the stairs. They keep me honest."

"Stop. Casey, stop trying to fix stuff. This is hard enough as it is."

I stopped talking. Took me a minute to realize that I'd said a thousand words for even one Tom had uttered. I turned back to him. His brown eyes didn't meet mine. The wind from Lake Erie blew his dark blond hair into his eyes, and no matter how many times he brushed it away, it moved back. Finally, he turned his back to the lake. I came around to stand in front of him. I grabbed his hands.

"Tell me." I gave his hands a little shake.

Whatever it was, we'd weather it together.

"I think we need to take a break."

"A break? How long? We're supposed to be moving in together in two weeks."

"We're not moving in. I just told you that."

"I'm not understanding. If your mom or uncle needs the house, I understand. It was a generous offer—"

"We shouldn't see each other anymore." He cut me off with those words, in more ways than one. "We're not right for each other. You need to meet someone who suits you better."

"I thought you suited me just fine."

"Please, let's make this as easy as possible. Tomorrow is going to be a long day."

"So, we're not going to be boyfriend and girlfriend anymore? No house, no bar trip, none of that?"

"It's been a great two years. You've been a champ. Congratulations. I hear you're graduating with honors, Order of the Coif and all that."

"None of that means anything without you."

"Casey, it means everything. Maybe I'll see you around," he said. I looked up and the sliding door was open. He was walking to the door. He was kicking me out. My boyfriend of two-and-a-half years was showing me the door.

"This is it. This is goodbye? Wait. Just tell me one thing. Why?" I didn't want to do the Effie thing. I didn't want to be the girl from the Motown musical I'd seen as a kid, who threw herself on the floor at the feet of a man. So I did nothing but follow him out the door, when he didn't answer. I stood on the front landing and watched my future evaporate in a puff of smoke.

"Whatever happens, you'll land on your feet. You're a great girl."

Tom closed the door. I was standing between six Doric columns I thought would welcome me home. They stood stoic, watching me, offering no solace. Mechanically, I walked into my car, opened the door, got in. I made it six blocks before I had to pull over because I couldn't see through the tears.

16

By the time my parents and I walked over to the Morrell Gates party, my feet were aching and my head was pounding. I promised myself I'd put in an appearance. Then I'd go home and hole up in my room for a day or ten while I recovered from the best and worst days of my life.

I'd tried hard to smile when the dean had placed the tasseled gold cords around my shoulders in recognition of graduating summa cum laude. I tried to share my parents' joy as they beamed from the back of the auditorium. I could see only one of my father's eyes. The other was covered by a video camera he'd used only two times, my college graduation being the first, this being the second. I knew he imagined my wedding being the third.

I hadn't told them a thing about Tom. I'd gone to North Moreland, not to pack, but to tell my tenant that I needed to be back in September, that he couldn't take over my lease. He had signed a lease in my building to move into another apartment, come January. I'd made the compromise deal knowing I could pay off my debts that much quicker if I were living at home.

Tomorrow, I'd tell my parents. They'd wonder why I wasn't packing. Why I wasn't moving in twelve days.

A large placard announced the entrance to the Morrell Gates party.

"This is nice," my mother said, tugging at her dress. I swatted her hands away.

"You look perfect, Mom. The wine colored wrap dress suits you."

It did. My mom looked a lot like the German beauty I imagine she had been when she'd caught my father's eye. A few pounds had rounded her out. But she still stood tall and straight, carrying her pride like a cloak. My father wasn't as sure of himself. He had never been comfortable at social occasions whether they were one of the few parties they'd ever had at our house or whether he was in the basement of St. Ignatius.

"Dad, why don't you and Mom get a little something to eat?" I pointed them toward the expansive buffet. I'd heard the eighties had been lavish, but the nineties buffet was no slouch. There were cold and hot foods, shrimp, crab, and oysters.

A prime rib bar was in one corner, a sundae bar in another. I hadn't fallen victim to the freshman fifteen, but I could see that I'd have to keep vigilant at firm functions. A fellow associate had told me that the late night dinners the firm ordered in when they were pulling all-nighters had made her suits a bit tight.

There was a bit of laughter and clinking of glasses in one corner of the ballroom.

I spotted the other Cleveland Marshall grad and walked over to him.

"What's all the toasting about?"

He looked at me oddly. "Did you read the invitation?"

"I was kind of busy with last minute law review stuff then, I just checked the 'yes' box."

"Oh, yeah. Heard about that. Sorry."

"No harm. No foul. We're all done with school. Now that we're here at Morrell I'll just put that all behind me. Anyway, you were saying. The invitation…"

"We're just window dressing. The main reason for the party is they're announcing the elevation of new partners. They've given speeches about two already. They're about to—"

Arthur Gates, Jr. tapped a fork on the side of a glass. It got quiet. I trained my eyes and ears toward him. I looked over to see that my parents were doing the same.

"Good evening, everyone. Tonight is a night of celebration. First, we're here to celebrate our newest associates. All of whom have graduated from law school in the last couple of weeks or will graduate very soon." Gates slipped a paper from his breast pocket. "Quiet please, while I read their names and their law schools."

I listened while he read the names of my fellow summer associates.

"Ah, I'm getting old, let me see if I can get these last two." He pulled reading glasses from the top of his head and affixed them to his nose. "Last but certainly not least we have, Patricia Ritchey of the University of Michigan and David Cummings from the Ohio State University. I hear that's a great school, by the way." Laughter filled the room. I waited a beat. Then two. I could feel the heat flood my face. I'd somehow been omitted from the list. I couldn't believe it. I looked over to find my parents whispering fiercely to each other.

I practically willed them not to say anything, sure it was an oversight. As soon as there was a lull, I'd get them to make a correction. By then the alcohol would have flowed and everyone would probably laugh even more.

I didn't get my chance. Not a minute later, Gates was silencing the room.

"We've already announced our new partners for Labor and Employment, Corporate and Tax. I'm especially proud to make this last announcement. Miriam Shively has been with the firm since nineteen eighty five." I looked around the room and spotted Miriam. This was amazing. My chest swelled with enough pride for the both of us.

She'd made it.

A woman who'd been sidelined had made it. I tuned back into Gates. "...has shown great initiative. In addition to carrying a full load of cases for our long term clients, Miriam is spearheading the litigation filed against Strohmeyer by the city of Brighthill. We're sure that Miriam and Ted will be a dynamic duo. Congratulations again Miriam, and welcome. I'm honored to call you my partner."

I clapped louder than anyone. After the applause subsided, a tuxedoed man sat down to a grand piano and started playing soft background music.

When all the backslapping and glass clinking was done, I approached Gates.

"Mr. Gates."

"Call me Art."

"Art, I was wondering if you'd be willing to make one last announcement adding me to the list of graduates." I fingered the tassel I'd been able to keep even though I'd returned the cap and gown. "I graduated summa cum laude today. Order of the Coif and everything."

Gates shifted from left to right as he grasped my elbow and moved me to an empty spot near a potted plant. "Did Miriam call you?"

"No, I don't think so," I said. "I'm happy for her, though. It's great that you've added a woman partner to your ranks. I hope to join her one day."

"So you didn't get a message from Miriam or her secretary?"

I looked up toward the dimmed ceiling lights as I thought about his question.

"Gah, no. But I sublet my apartment for the summer, and the guy who took it over is away for the weekend. Between getting ready for graduation and finishing up my last exam, I haven't had time to keep up on any messages. Why?"

"Let's step out into the hall."

"Okay," I said, allowing Gates to steer me into a quiet hallway. Its silence stood in stark contrast to the boisterous party in the ballroom.

"There's no easy way to say this."

Trepidation made my ankles wobble. I struggled to stay tall in my red peep toe pumps. I balled up my hands so I didn't pull at the dress that suddenly seemed all wrong.

"We had a partners meeting last week. In addition to voting on new partners, we did a reassessment of our department needs—"

"Litigation was my first choice," I interrupted. "But I'm glad to go wherever I'm needed."

"Thanks for your flexibility, Casey. It will stand you in good stead. Unfortunately, our staffing needs are met. We'll be rescinding our offer. But a woman like you, summa cum laude, with all those great skills, should have no problem finding a position. Any firm would be lucky to have you."

"So, you don't need me to start in September? Will there be any openings come January, or would I be able to start with the next class?" I may have not been Effie yesterday, but the urge to claw back what I was losing was greater today.

"A clean break is best, Casey. We don't want to hold you back. You're very employable. And while our needs might change, you would be best served to start looking now or after you've passed the bar exam. Sorry to give you the news like this, but we wish you the best of luck."

With that, Gates turned on his heel and marched back into the party. A loud 'Huzzah' came through the door like he was some long lost general coming back from battle abroad. The door closed and I was alone in the hallway.

Morrell Gates had rescinded their offer.

Come September I was unemployed.

Come June I wasn't moving in with Tom.

Not caring who saw, I let tears fall. How in the hell had my life imploded in two months? Sixty days ago, I'd been on top of the world. I looked down. Now, I had nothing but this stupid tasseled gold rope hanging around my neck.

I swiped away the tears with my hand then headed in the room. I pulled a plate of Swedish meatballs from my mother and a napoleon from my father and deposited them on cocktail tables.

"Mom, Dad, we have to go."

"Lieb, that was rude. We were eating—"

"We have to go. Now!" I whisper-shouted. They finally twigged, and I heard the heavy footfalls of my parents follow me from the room, out of the hotel, and on the long walk to the lot where we they'd parked their car.

"Casey Ann Cort," my father said as he turned the key in the ignition. "We've raised you better than this. Why—"

"They took back their job, Papa, that's why. And Mama, you were right. Tom doesn't want to marry me. As a matter of fact, he wants nothing to do with me. Let's go home before my head explodes."

They both looked at me with wary eyes, but didn't say anything further on the ride from east side to west.

17

"Merry Christmas, girl!" Lulu ran through the restaurant to give me a big hug. I'm sure we scared the shit out of the owners with all the screaming and hugging.

"What should I wish for you?" I asked. Catholic girl plus Jewish friend equaled awkward. Twelve years of Catholic education hadn't taught me much about what to say to people who celebrated non-Christian holidays.

"Shit. Merry Christmas. Happy Holidays. Whatever. Just don't pummel with me a Happy Hanukah. I swear some people around here treat it like it's Jewish Christmas. I want to say, peeps, it's okay, my people don't have to do the big pagan ritual to be happy."

"Happy Kwanzaa, then."

"You've gone and got funny in the last six months."

We sat down to lunch and Lulu snagged the waitress and ordered the regular.

"How's it going?" I asked. For a brief moment, I wanted to live vicariously through my friend. See the world as it was supposed to have been for me.

"Pretty cool. I'm really digging Dalton Lacey so far. We went to a Cavaliers/Raptors game on Tuesday. Our baseball team is better. Can't wait until we get some proper basketball players up in this town. The client was pretty cool though. I'm working on some neat stuff. I may even get to travel to Rotterdam for a month. A partner has a big international arbitration there and needs a cheap associate. If I get to go to the Netherlands, I'll be as cheap as they come."

"Sounds great," I said, trying and failing to inject enthusiasm into my voice.

"Oh shit, Casey, I'm sorry. How's it going? Anything pan out with the Security and Exchange commission in DC?"

"I'm glad to hear things are going well for you, seriously. Please tell me more. I didn't want lunch to turn into a one-woman pity party. And no, the SEC isn't interested in taking me on. Turns out they have plenty of Ivy League graduates to choose from."

"Case, I wish I could help out more. But as a first year at Dalton I'm low Jew on the totem pole."

"Mixed metaphor."

"Yeah, I know. So you've got nothing in the works as far as interviews?"

"All I get are form rejections, or 'we're not hiring' or the worst, nothing at all. I think I'm all out of ideas and I'm not up for taking a new bar exam in February and trying my luck elsewhere."

"What are you going to do?"

"I'm kind of thinking about hanging out a shingle. The phonebook is full of people who seem to be supporting themselves in private practice. I even met with a couple of lawyers who thought I could make a go of it."

"What do your mom and dad say?"

"They think it's a wonderful idea, of course. I talked to them about it while filling out my loan deferment forms at the kitchen table. I love them, Lulu, I do. But I don't think they get it. As far as they're concerned, I'm already a success. A seventy thousand dollar in debt loser, but a success nonetheless. They think I've achieved the American dream."

"Maybe they're kind of right though. No one can fire you from the Law Offices of Casey Cort."

"I tried calling Tom last night," I admitted quietly between sips of hot tea.

"There's never going to be the closure you want, hon. You know that, right?"

"He changed his number." The mechanical operator voice had been a punch in the gut. "I called and it was no longer in service. I don't even have a number for him."

"What do you think talking to him will get you?"

"I have to know if his family and the Strohmeyers blackballed me. If he ever really loved me. I don't know. But the blackball thing mostly. Honestly, I kinda thought being a summa cum laude graduate would open if not all the doors, at least some of them."

"I think that skank Miriam Shively was the one who did you in. She probably sold you out. Too much of a coincidence for me that one minute she was moaning about not making partner, then the next, she's the head of the Strohmeyer legal defense team with a partner salary and corner office to boot."

Those facts I'd shared with her from the gossip mill. I kind of wished that my friends from Morrell didn't feel the need to fill me in from their brand new e-mail accounts. I shook my head, trying to clear it. I'd gone over and over all of it in my head a thousand times while sitting at my childhood desk drafting resumes and cover letters, while driving around Ohio, Pennsylvania and DC going to job interviews.

"I don't know who or what is working against me. But I can't sit on my parents' couch for another six months trying to figure it out."

"It's a shitty market. You know that. Half our class was unemployed at graduation. I'm working on any project at any hour these Dalton Lacey guys wish so I can keep my job. We're all disposable. You just got it earlier than the rest. You know most associates wash out."

I practically sighed in appreciation when the food arrived. Chow fun, how I'd missed it.

"Finally something that's not full of sour cream. My mother's killing me with the food."

"So move out. Get your apartment back. Get a cat or a dog. Declare your independence."

"Seriously?"

"You can't let a single setback get you down. There'll be another job. There'll be another guy. That perfect life you'd built up with Tom in your head ain't happening. Honestly, you should be happy to find out the whole thing was a sham before you got married. You'd hate to be dumped three years and three kids in."

"At least I'd get alimony and child support," I grumbled, thinking about my pitiful bank balance.

"Casey. I know it doesn't seem like it. But I think it's going to be okay. Let me get lunch and as a Christmas gift,

I'll buy your business cards. They'll be on me. I want to be the first to hold a Law Offices of Casey Cort card in my hand."

I tried my best not to cry. There'd been entirely too much of that lately.

"Happy holidays to you, too."

18

"Hi, I'm Justin McPhee." I looked up to see a guy, a little bit older than me, holding out his hand. His brown eyes were warm and friendly. I didn't get the least hitting on me vibe from him, so I smiled back. Then I took the card proffered, and shook his warm hand. "You?" he asked.

"Casey Cort," I answered.

"This seat free?"

I was the only person at the round six-person table. We were in the conference room of the county bar association. The dark blue tablecloth had been covered by branded three-ring binders, a stylized courthouse logo in the middle of each. I'd been just about to open the notebook when McPhee had approached.

"Sure. Have a seat," I offered, not able to think of a reason to turn him down.

"You got a card?" he asked.

Took me a moment to realize what he was asking for. I'd only given one card out, to Lulu as promised. They'd arrived in the mail just this week to my new office in the Huntington Building on East Ninth Street and Euclid Avenue. His face was expectant, so I opened my purse and pulled out one of the cream-colored cards.

"Law Offices of Casey Cort," he read aloud. "Haven't heard of you. Just hung out your shingle, yeah?"

I bit my lip then nodded. "Started January first."

McPhee hunched forward, his brown eyes were intense. "You didn't want to go into private practice?"

Obvious, I was. I'd need to be less easy to read in the future, otherwise other lawyers would bury me alive, eat me for breakfast, all the clichés.

"I was supposed to be at Morrell Gates last fall," I blurted out before I could stop myself. I wondered when the day would come where that wouldn't sting so badly.

"Is that so? There are a lot of stories like that floating around."

"What do you mean?"

"Half the people you meet probably didn't enter law school thinking they'd be a sole practitioner in private practice on the back end. We're all of us Common Pleas Lawyers now."

"That true for you?"

"Sure. I graduated from Case. Got a job clerking for Judge Morris down in Akron. Six months into my clerkship, Judge Morris kicked the bucket. I had my bar certificate in hand, half a year at a prestigious job under my belt. I'd be fine I figured. Worked as a staff attorney for the remaining months and applied for jobs everywhere. Thought law firms would be kicking down my door to hire a former clerk.

"But a dead judge holds no sway. When I ran out of money, I started doing favors for my parents' friends, my neighbors and the like. Started borrowing conference room space for meetings. My roommate got tired of taking messages for me, so I got a small office in the Standard Building. Here I am two years later."

"I looked in the Standard Building. You on the sixth floor?"

"In the pink palace." It was a much kinder description than the one I'd heard from the office manager who'd shown it to me. He'd called the office that lent space to dozens of lawyers, titty pink, and he hadn't been wrong. Crass, but not wrong. The space had been expensive and crowded. I'd picked an empty supply closet another firm was renting out. Quiet, no view, but cheap.

"What are you doing?" he asked, keeping the conversation going where I would have checked out.

"Everything that comes in the door," I said. I didn't tell him that nothing more than a few wills from my parents' parish friends had come through said door. "I'm here to do this training so I can add more stable work to the balance."

This training was to become a Guardian ad Litem in Juvenile Court. A couple of attorneys I'd met filing the wills down in probate had suggested it. Said it was a way to pay my dues and pay my bills. I'd done the calculations in my head dozens of times. If I could get ten cases a month, I could pay my rent on my office and my apartment. Extra living expenses and student loans? That would have to wait.

"What do you want to do?" he asked. "I mean really?"

I didn't answer out loud, but the answers were obvious. Get my old life back. Go to work in a tall building with pretty views and secretarial help.

"Anything except personal injury, social security, and worker's comp, probably," I finally said. It had been a long day paging through the phonebook, figuring out what lawyers did outside law firms and government. "I don't have the expertise for medical issues nor can I front the money for those cases."

"I hear that. You got a pen?"

I opened my purse again and took out a ballpoint. McPhee lifted one of the scratch pads from the middle of the table. "I'm gonna do you the favor I wish someone had done for me."

"What am I going to owe you?" This was a you scratch mine, I'll scratch yours town, and I didn't have any more scratches left in me.

"Nothing. Maybe a drink at the Lincoln Inn one of these days." He started writing. "Look, these GAL cases are steady, I hear, but there's a bucket of other appointed work you can add to your plate. Keeps it interesting, and keeps the money coming in. The government may pay slow, but they always pay. First, there's criminal defense."

"Wait. What? Cuyahoga County has a public defender. I met him at a party."

"Well Ms. High Brow, I can't say I've ever met him at any party, but the rules require that sixty-five percent of cases are assigned to the private bar. The public defender's office has maybe forty, fifty lawyers, the rest go to us."

"Seriously. I just sign up?"

"Not that easy. You have to get some trial experience, fill out an application, and get on the candy list."

"Candy list?"

"It's a pay to play system. If you can slip a few donations to the judge's reelection campaigns, you get more assignments."

"Been open all of eleven days, I'm not exactly rolling in the dough here."

"You're a girl. If I were you, I'd hit up a couple of sympathetic judges. Take your card, talk to the judge in person, ask for a couple of low-level felonies. Did you go to Cleveland Marshall?" At my nod, he continued. "Maybe one of your professors can put in a word with a judge or two. Each judge does two weeks in the room. That's one."

"There's more?"

The speakers were starting to shuffle near the front of the room, but I was starting to think that what McPhee was saying was far more important.

"Mediation, fifty a case, but it's like an hour out of your afternoon, when you'd been jonesing for a pop anyway. Guardian in Domestic Relations is about a thousand from a bond posted up front, but can be more depending on how much the couple has. Plus with your credentials, you can get assigned appeals. I'd start with Juvy, those are seven fifty. Felonies are a thousand. There are less judges to hit up in the eighth district too."

A woman tapped the microphone at the front of the room.

"Get the county bar deskbook. Read it cover to cover. You're a smart girl, you'll figure it out."

"People always say there are too many lawyers," the speaker started, and I hastened to turn off all the information I'd just received and tune into her. "Maybe that's true for the rich, but not for the poor. We thank you for volunteering to spend your day with us. We at the Guardian ad Litem project thank you in advance for taking on the defenseless clients who need you most. Let's get started.

"In Juvenile Court, we have abuse, neglect, and dependency on the one hand," the woman said, "and the best interests of the child on the other. Ohio Revised Code sections twenty-one fifty-one will become your best friend. Read it, memorize it, and apply it. I suggest you get Ohio juvenile law treatise," she held up a doorstop-thick paperback with a blue marbled cover, "and keep it with you when you come to Common Pleas Court."

I took a brand new yellow legal pad from the briefcase my parents had bought for my graduation and started taking notes with the gold Cross pens they'd added to the pocket as a bonus. If this was going to be my life, if I was going to be a Common Pleas Lawyer, I needed to stop feeling sorry for myself and start paying attention.

19

Jenny Nolan was like my new best friend. Every few days
since I'd completed the day-long training, the Juvenile
Court assignment clerk called asking if I wanted new cases.
Looking around my office, bare save for two framed diplomas and nothing but a whole lot of time, I always said yes.
I even said yes when she asked if I'd take juvenile crimes.
They didn't pay much either, but I reasoned it would be a
good idea to get some experience on lower stakes cases before going hat in hand to the judges who handled felony
cases to try to get on that so-called candy list.

I was transferring the names Jenny had given me this
week to the tabs of empty manila folders when my phone
rang. I pressed speaker to answer the internal call from the
receptionist all the lawyers in the suite shared.

"Casey, there's a woman to see you. She says she's your two o'clock appointment."

"Send her back. Thanks."

"Are you Penny Canaday?" I asked the young girl who hesitated by the door after the receptionist left. She nodded, but didn't move. "Please come in," I said, motioning the girl in. She moved cautiously. Finally, I rose, pulled out one of the two chairs I'd purchased at a flea market, and closed the door for both quiet and privacy.

I was probably as nervous as she was. I would never tell her, but she was the first client to step foot into my office. I had no idea if I'd be able to help her, but I asked anyway.

"How can I help you?"

"You look young. You a real attorney?" Canaday said.

I sat up a little straighter and looked at her a little closer. There was something about her voice that was, I don't know, off. Kind of reminded me of a student exchange we'd done with the St. Rita School for the Deaf when I'd been a junior or senior at St. Joseph.

"I am a real attorney," I said, glancing back at the framed diplomas behind me. "Graduated with honors and every-thing. The file the court sent over said you were charged with felony theft from Mega Mart on Brookpark Road?"

Canaday leaned forward, but didn't answer.

"Are you hearing impaired?"

"Yes," she nodded vigorously.

"Can you hear me now?"

"For the most part. If you could maybe talk louder and slower, I could follow you."

I did as she asked and discovered she'd taken her little sister shopping at Mega Mart for a winter coat. Somehow, the little girl had picked up a Buzz Lightyear doll that had been sold out a couple of months before. Canaday had thought she'd put the toy on layaway, but the clerk told her she could take it. Once outside the store, security had rounded them up, then cops had come and arrested her.

"Could you actually hear all of what the cashier said?"

Canaday shook her head.

"Do you have a hearing aid?"

"The school gives me one when I'm there, but I have to return it at the end of the year. I didn't get it back after Christmas because I didn't go back."

"Wait. I want to be sure I'm understanding you clearly," I said. "You can only have the hearing aid when you're at school."

Canaday nodded, her head bobbing longer than most. I looked at my two or three lines of notes and didn't have the first clue as to how to help her.

"I tell you what. You give me a few days, maybe a week to look into this and we'll meet before your court date on the twenty-third."

The minute Canaday walked out the door, I pulled out what was turning out to be my greatest resource, the phone book.

February 23, 1997

Penny Canaday was practically bouncing on her toes when I met her on the steps of the Juvenile Courthouse on East Twenty-Second Street. We cleared security together, and I took her to a corner of the stone and marble foyer, hoping our voices didn't bounce too much and I could maintain a little confidentiality.

"How are you?"

I received an impromptu hug instead of an answer to my question.

"Are you ready to go in? We're scheduled in ten minutes."

Canaday nodded. I left her on one of the church-style pew benches and announced our arrival for the clerk. She looked down at her notes and told me that we could go on in to the courtroom as we were the first case. I backed out of the small room and motioned for my client to come forward.

"We're first today. I'd hoped to get more time to talk to you. We have a deal with the prosecutor to dismiss your case if you don't commit any crimes over the next six months. You think that would work?"

"Yes. Sure. I just want to get back to school."

The judge's bailiff called our case and we all stepped forward toward the tables. Once we were assembled, the bailiff pressed two buttons on a tape recorder to get the hearing on the record.

"Good afternoon, Ms. Cort is it? Your high bar number tells me you're new." I nodded, a little embarrassed to be called out as inexperienced on my first day in court. "We're glad to see you here. Shows that you take your responsibility to handle matters for the indigent seriously."

"Thank you, Your Honor."

"We're here in the matter of Penny Canaday, a minor child. Ms. Canaday, you've been charged with theft from Mega Mart. The prosecutor informs me that we've come to an agreement, is that correct?"

Both the prosecutor and I nodded. My biggest fear had been that I'd be up against Tom in one of my first cases. I shouldn't have worried, though. The gossip in the courthouse was that Tom got to skip the grunt work assignment of Juvenile Court and was in training for felony cases right off the bat. Somehow, that little nugget of information had felt like both a blessing and a curse. I tuned the judge back in.

"Ms. Cort, can you tell me a little bit about the case?"

"My client is Penny Canaday. She's sixteen years old. She was born with a severe hearing impairment. The school that she attends provides hearing aids for students, but when she dropped out at the end of the semester to help take care of her sister while her parents worked three jobs apiece, she lost the use of the school-provided hearing aid.

"What we have here is a case of a severe misunderstanding that was escalated to a criminal matter. When I met with the prosecutor, I advised him I was going to file a motion to suppress my client's confession to police because during the time of the arrest and subsequent questioning, she was unable to hear, understand, or knowingly waive her constitutional rights. I provided evidence, which I've also shared with the court, outlining Ms. Canaday's hearing impairment. Unfortunately, the same impairment caused a misunderstanding with the cashier at Mega Mart concerning layaway of the toy purchase."

"Ms. Canaday, can you hear what your lawyer has said?"

"Yes, Your Honor. Miss Cort called Social Services and got me a hearing test. They hooked me up with a place that provided this hearing aid free of charge. It's really good, Judge. There's no buzzing like the school one. Do you know, when I walked home from the bus stop that I was able to hear birds for the first time? Did you know birds made noise? They chirp and sing and stuff. I heard cars coming and kids playing in the park. The world is filled with sound. It's wonderful."

"Thank you, Ms. Canaday. Having reviewed the facts in evidence before me, I agree to the plea agreement reached by the parties. The case against Penny Canaday is hereby dismissed. The dismissal is stayed for six months from the date of judgment entry. If no further action comes before this court against Ms. Canaday, the case will be dismissed with prejudice. Do you understand and agree to the terms of this dismissal, Ms. Canaday?"

"Yes, Your Honor. I've never been in trouble before. My mom caught a break with day care, which Ms. Cort helped out with, so I can start school back on Monday."

"That's good news, Ms. Canaday." The judge looked back and forth between Canaday, me and the prosecutor. "Anything else?" When no one answered, she banged the gavel. "It is so ordered."

I started to shove the client's folder back in my bag. Canaday was talking rapidly in my ear about her excitement at getting her diploma in June if she made up her missed work. The hearing aid had turned her into a chatterbox.

"Off the record, counselors," the judge said. Immediately I stopped what I was doing and turned my attention back to the bench. If I'd learned one thing in that seminar, it was that the judge was king or queen of their courtroom domain.

"Yes, Your Honor," the prosecutor and I said simultaneously.

"Casey Cort, I hope to see more of you here. You're an asset to the bar and Common Pleas Court. You've gone above and beyond and are to be commended. Thank you."

I could feel heat stealing up my face. I mumbled my own thanks into my chest. I'd have to tell my mom and her friends about this at service on Sunday. They'd all be very proud.

A weight lifted, and my heart was lighter than it had been in months. Maybe being a Common Pleas Lawyer wouldn't be so bad.

ABOUT THE AUTHOR

Aime Austin is the author of the Casey Cort Legal Thriller Series. Casey is almost always in trouble. Aime's full time job? Rescuing her. Good thing Aime's got experience. She practiced family and criminal law in Cleveland, Ohio for several years—so she has the skills for the job.

When Aime isn't rescuing Casey from herself, she's raising her son or traveling between Budapest and Los Angeles.